Fleeting As Sunset

Fifty or So One Minute Stories

BY

FREDDA J. BURTON

ALSO BY FREDDA J. BURTON

Historical Fiction

The Chocolate Set: A Swedish Journey
Ellis Island to the Last Best West

Short Stories

War and Storm
Way Too Many Goodbyes

Non Fiction

Only the Destination Was Wrong: Hanson-Persson Family
History

Numerous Articles and Illustrations In
Mother Earth News
Countryside Magazine
Tidepools
Outdoor Illinois Magazine
Various Scientific Books and Journals
[Such as:
Forest Trees of Illinois
American Fern Journal
Illinois and Regional Plant Guides
Flora of Illinois]

Introduction

These are "one minute stories" after a traditional form of writing popular in Chinese literature. The one minute story can be traced back to ancient times. 770-207 B.C. to be exact. Pre-Quin essays, fairy tales from the Wei and Jin dynasties, legends of the Ming and Qing dynasties all used this form of expression.

The one minute story seems suited to the fast paced, many faceted life style of today. Like life, these short, short stories are made up from the cloth of reality. Cut and stitched from dozens of happenings, memories, and tales told by friend and stranger alike.

A story is new cloth made from rags. Recycled words and memories. Some are factual, some are not, but all of them are TRUE.

For My Husband, Theodore A Burton

I. THE GOOD OLD DAYS

Return To Bison 1942

Just a few days after their first wedding anniversary in June of 1908, Hilma and Charles Hanson boarded a train at Sioux Falls, South Dakota and headed west, part of the last great migration. At the end of the rail line they transferred their baggage to a wagon driven by Charlie's brother who had gone on ahead a few months earlier. Their destination was a homestead a few miles from the settlement of Coal Springs.

A sod house had already been carved from the untouched prairie. They moved their collection of belongings into the bare dirt walled soddy and set about making it home. Though there is no record of it, I'm sure Hilma wept while she hung blankets and bolts of material on the walls to keep the mess out of her domain. She unpacked the China chocolate set she had received as a wedding present from her family in Sweden and placed it on a small round table she had covered with a velvet cloth. A curtain divided the bedroom from the rest of the house. She made up a bed on a narrow platform of sod with the feather tick and home sewed quilts.

She demanded great care be taken when the men unloaded her rocking chair and the bent wood straight chair. She was probably frantic when her precious sewing machine slipped from her brother-in-law's grasp as he hauled it from the wagon. Fortunately it escaped with only a scratch.

Before long, an array of pictures were pinned to the coverings on the soddy walls. Photographs and magazine cut outs, even a few childish drawings from nieces and nephews back in Sioux Falls. She served tea from the delicate chocolate pot to the other homestead wives who called on her and contemplated her advancing pregnancy in her spare time. Her husband on the other hand raced around the county with the other young bucks, target shooting, rock climbing, and ogling a neighbor's new car, the first in the county.

Well, Charlie got his car and Hilma had three babies in the sod house. They proved up their claim, then sold the sod house with its barren acreage and moved to town. They built a house or two, opened a store that included an ice cream parlor, and got Charlie elected County Clerk. His term complete, Charlie tried his hand as sheriff for a couple of years. The three babies became six and the Hansons decided to migrate south to the northern edge of the Black Hills where trees and green grass replaced the dry dust of Perkins County. Charlie became a real estate agent. Another baby joined the original six.

Over the years friends from Bison ventured south to visit the Hansons and vice-versa. One year Charlie and friends hauled the antique Deadwood stage to Bison for the Old Timers parade. None of the family seemed interested in visiting the old soddy.

In the fall of 1942, September 6th to be exact, the family not involved in the war effort made the drive from Spearfish to Bison. Hilma and Charlie, two daughters, and a grandbaby squeezed into the old Chevy for the long, hot drive.

They were met by old friends and offered overnight accommodations, a dozen supper invitations, and a lot of catching up on friends and family news. The reminiscing lasted long into the night. Local friends were anxious to show their visitors some new additions to the town.

In addition to the new school and a bowling alley a sense of history had awakened in the next generation. The old one room jail house had been spruced up and a plaque with some words of history added. The first sod house in the county had been transformed into a museum of local history. Old rifles, dishes, rude furniture, harness, tools, and photographs were displayed inside. Several old wagons and the doctor's buggy were arranged out front.

The visit to the sod house museum sparked a conversation about a visit to the old Hanson family soddy. The older generation, the grandparents expressed a complete lack of interest and Hilma declared she would never, ever set foot in that place again. The daughters were very interested in seeing the old home place and the birthplace of their older siblings.

The group, minus Hilma, set out to find the homestead on the grassy prairie outside of town. With much argument they found a dim track marked more for its different vegetation, than any feat of memory. Solid ground fit for a car lasted until they were nearly a mile from the county road.

From there they walked until they found a large pile of rocks used as a section marker in the old days. Certain they were in the right place, they continued on until Charlie called a halt. Standing in the waist high grass he declared this to be the place. They took turns snapping photos and used a few more minutes to search for any signs of the old house. The prairie it seemed had obliterated everything. The heat soon forced them back to the car.

That was the last visit those original homesteaders made to Bison. Life intervened. Gas rationing, nursing school, babies, illness and death pushed that part of family history into the background. It wasn't until the turn of the century that anyone thought about a trip north.

In 2008 a group of grandchildren, cousins, made the trip north. The road was much improved, but the filling station at the half way point looked the same with its old glass topped pumps and a pop cooler in back near the outhouses. A 'no gas' sign hung on the pumps and a jar in the pop cooler received our quarters. No sign of an attendant.

In Bison we visited the town's first sod house. It had been enclosed in a clapboard structure to prevent it from melting away. Inside we found wash tubs, scrub boards, rusted traps, and old rifles. And a mess of cob webs and spiders. The museum itself had been moved to a nearby block building.

At the museum we found a display from the junior class at the old high school. It included a dress made by our oldest aunt in 1924. Pretty slim pickings. We snapped a few pictures, then headed for the court house to look up the registration records for the homesteads. The information was sparse but lined up with all we had been told over the years.

We drove back to Spearfish with a sense that we knew all that was knowable about that chapter of our history.

Victory Garden 1943

Slogans in abundance marked 1943. Many of them addressed the problem of food shortages. Posters and pamphlets urged everyone to get out and garden. The British had some of the most inventive of the slogans and such encouragements as 'Our Food Is Fighting' and 'Dig For Victory' were borrowed for posters in the United States.

Vacant lots, front lawns, and waste space were commandeered for planting. My grandfather, Charlie, was involved in the movement in Spearfish. He had sold real estate before the depression and knew just about everyone in town. He had no trouble recruiting volunteers. His own personal project was the wide strip of land next door to the house he was building on University Avenue.

He had trouble finding a tractor for the initial ground breaking, then the county came through with a program to loan a machine and operator for the job. With the heavy work finished a group of volunteers spent a weekend removing rocks, roots, and old concrete from the quarter acre. By the spring of 1943 the ground was ready for planting.

By May of 1943 there were 18 million Victory gardens in the United States. Even Eleanor Roosevelt reassigned a portion of the White House lawn to plant tomatoes and sweet corn. A third of the vegetables grown in the country came from Victory Gardens.

Charlie Hanson and his friend, Ralph Stordahl, along with relatives too young or too old to serve in the military put the finishing touches on the garden. They mounded and mulched earth for tomato plants and squash, hoed soil into raised rows for corn, and beans. A pile of old trellis stood ready to hold the peas and other climbing plants and watering cans stood ready at the pump in case of a dry spell. Now for the planting.

A trip to Lown's General Store for seed and starter plants was a bit disappointing. When they asked for five pounds of onion sets in mixed varieties, Mr. Lown said 'Sorry, they only sent yellow on my last order.' Radish and carrot seed was totally unavailable and not likely to show up this season.

Undaunted, Charlie and Ralph went home with a trunk load of seed potatoes, corn, turnip, rutabagas, lettuce, bean and squash seed, tomato plants and even a few herbs to flavor things up.

There were plenty of volunteers for the planting, not so many for weeding and upkeep. On April 27th the local newspaper printed a notice that read in part: *'Attention. Because of the urgent necessity of all Spearfish Victory Gardens producing the maximum food in this year of the war, all owners of chickens and dogs are requested to keep them penned or otherwise contained so that they can do no damage to vegetable gardens....your cooperation in this matter will be of much assistance in helping us all do our part to grow more food for quicker victory. By order of the City Council.'*

This warning was repeated many times in the 'Queen City Mail,' the Spearfish newspaper, along with the names of offending parties.

The gardens flourished until the night of May 13th when snow and freezing temperatures nipped the more tender plants into early death. Not to be thwarted, Ralph and Charlie paid another visit to Lown's General Store only to be told that no seed was available. Mr. Lown also warned the gardeners that wide mouth canning jars were no longer in stock and regular canning supplies would soon follow suit. 'Buy now,' he warned. But on the bright side he told the two men to pass on the fact to their women folk that he had 'received a shipment of 30 dozen pairs of rayon hose' which he was offering at 69 cents a pair.

They scoured the county for more seed and put the word out that starts and cuttings of anything edible would be welcome in the new garden. Many a housewife scrounged up a half used pack of seeds from the year before and others brought rooted shoots of quince and gooseberry. A few parted with precious strawberry plants. The garden was quickly restored and the new plantings flourished.

By fall 8 million tons of food had been harvested from the Victory gardens across the country, a third of all food production in America. The gardens and gardeners really got going in the spring of 1944 and nearly equaled commercial production across the country. Unfortunately, Grandpa Charlie did not live to see this achievement. He died in May 25, 1944 at age 63.

The Victory Gardens continued to produce food in record amounts through the end of the war. With the return of troops attention moved on to things like housing and jobs. Food production dwindled and shortages surged until the early 1950's when commercial production finally ramped up to pre-war levels.

8

Rhubarb and Ration Books

Sugar was the first food to be rationed in the United States during World War II. War with Japan cut off sugar imports from the Philippines and cargo ships from Hawaii were diverted to military purposes. It was a boon to sugar beet growers, but it takes time to plow and plant and raise a crop to maturity, harvest the beets, haul them to the plant, and process them into sugar.

In the spring of 1942 the first sugar coupon books were ready for distribution to every citizen. Theoretically each person was allowed one pound of sugar every two weeks, but often no sugar at all could be found in the stores. Sugar did not return to normal levels until 1947.

If all a person did was to spoon a bit of sugar into their coffee cup or sprinkle it on a bowl of shredded wheat, rationing had little effect on normal life. However, the house wives of western South Dakota had a much greater agenda when it came to sugar. Canning, baking, and making jam, jelly, and candy was a normal part of life. As food supplies in the stores dwindled, these activities became more and more important.

My grandmother, Hilma, had a huge garden and a small house. By the middle of 1942 my mother and I had moved in with her because my dad was in Honolulu working on the new underground fuel tanks to replace those destroyed in the December attack in1941. It was also the summer of the most enormous crop of both rhubarb and gooseberries we had ever seen.

Rhubarb and gooseberries are probably the sourest fruit known to man. Mouth puckering sour. They need sugar. Lots and lots of sugar to convert their flesh into pies and jams and mouth watering sauces. And our collective sugar allotment was three pounds every two weeks. A drop in the bucket.

Since the person using a sugar stamp was required to be present and the seller was required to remove the stamp from the ration book, it made trading stamps difficult. The only possible excuse for a loose stamp was the flimsy nature of the ration books.

My dad mailed his sugar coupons from Hawaii and Mom would stick them in my ration book. Who would dare question the smile of a little kid handing a tattered book to a store clerk anyway. She also roped her sister and niece into her sugar gathering scheme by promising them a portion of the end product. At least they could hand over their ration books in person.

As the rhubarb did its part by growing thick sturdy stalks and the gooseberries ripened and bent the branches of the bushes lower and lower, the hoard of sugar grew. When it reached a good level, we hauled the big canning kettle up from the cellar, washed jars and assembled lids and rings. Hilma's small kitchen looked like a mini cannery.

We washed and chopped the rhubarb and gave it a preliminary boil to help it absorb the maximum amount of the precious sugar. Packed in jars it went into the water bath for processing. We gathered up the huge pile of discarded tops and tossed them into the chicken yard. Turns out chickens don't like rhubarb leaves and we had to gather them again for the trash pile.

The gooseberries followed the same path as the rhubarb, though picking the leaves and stems from the little berries was a tedious job. After the first flush of canning wound up we got creative and mixed the chopped rhubarb with the gooseberries.

The following week the tail end of the gooseberries ripened and became pie. The rhubarb was still going strong. Unfortunately you could see the bottom of the sugar canister. Even if another round of sugar stamps were activated, the store shelves were empty. As hard as we tried we couldn't find a substitute sweetener. The last inch in the syrup bottle was no help, honey, even if we had some, did not process well. Candy and gum had disappeared from store shelves. Our sweet tooth would remain unappeased.

We tried to give away the last of the rhubarb crop, but no one else had sugar either. As a consolation my mother snapped a photo of Hilma with her neighbor ladies holding great arm loads of rhubarb. Film, itself, would be rationed and then become totally unavailable in another year. We left the last couple of bushels on the plants to grow old and tough and woody. We did have enough stored up on the cellar shelves to last several years. We talked about the wasted crop for years.

12

13

The Tailless Cat

Many, many houses in Lead, South Dakota had been boarded up and let to sit empty when the gold mine closed, closed by the government in 1942. The Anderson clan's houses were no exception. Brothers and brother-in-law had left town by September, some to the draft, some to enlist, and one to escape such high danger stuff. Ivar, the daddy of the clan, was last to be laid off on Christmas Eve.

He finished boarding up the five houses and took off for San Pedro, California to find work. Lead became a ghost town.

The houses sat unattended through several harsh winters, pounding rain of spring and fall, heat of summer. The trees and bushes grew as did the grass and weeds. By the time the mine reopened the houses were invisible from the street because of the thick growth.

My dad, fresh home from the Navy, decided to move us into one of the Lead houses while he waited for his GI Bill education to begin in the fall of 1946. Free rent and, besides, the house needed attention. More than he could have known.

He enlisted his brother-in-law to help with cutting enough of the brush to reach the front door and make a path around the house. They removed the boards from the windows and piled the debris in the side yard. My mom and her sisters arrived to clean. They scrubbed windows and floors while the men made a beer run and on their return the party began.

A few more weekends of this feverish work and wild partying made the old house good as new. Almost.

We moved our table and beds and lamps and radio into the house. The kitchen came to life with dishes and toaster, knives and forks. The fridge needed some work, but before long my dad had it humming along. All seemed well until my mom spotted a giant rat peering out from behind the cellar door. We hustled back to my grandma's house in Spearfish where a big discussion of rat removal took center stage.

An old Finnish neighbor finally suggested a cat and said she had just the right one. A gray stripy tom without a tail. A special breed she said. None of them have tails, but they are quick to pounce and don't let go. Ten bucks changed hands and we returned to Lead with the cat in the back seat. He was a friendly thing and seemed to know that he was about to go to work.

And he did. Purring pet by day, monster hunter at night. By the time warm weather arrived he had racked up a couple of dozen kills and the remaining rats found sanctuary in another empty house.

Unfortunately the warm weather and the warm house hatched out a new problem. Bugs—lice, fleas, bed bugs, ants, roaches, and earwigs. We went to bed slapping creepy crawling things and we woke up scratching. Old Tailless wasn't going to be much help with this varmint problem. He was scratching himself raw right along with us.

Bug spray, bug bombs, and more cleaning had little effect. We finally called an exterminator from Rapid City. After his examination of our house he said he figured tenting and fumigating was the only solution short of torching the place.

We made plans to spend the night at Grandma's and watched the bug ridding crew inflate a big tent affair over our house. Twenty-four hours should do the job they warned as they hooked up hoses to inject the poison gas into the house.

A little later we noticed the cat was missing. Must still be in the house, muttered my dad. Stop pumping, he shouted to the exterminator crew. With a handkerchief over his nose and mouth he unsnapped the tent door and ran into the foggy house.

The crew turned off the compressor and we all stood on the curb trying to imagine what was happening inside the house. After what seemed like a very long time my dad staggered out of the tent with limp old Tailless draped over his arm.

We cheered and then helped the exterminator crew hold an oxygen mask for my dad. He took it off after a few gulps of air and put it to the cat's face. A minute or ten later the cat shuddered and coughed, then opened his eyes, shook himself, and stood up. We all cheered.

Extermination continued and in a few days we had a bug-less house and a slightly subdued cat who went back to patrolling for rats. The rest of the summer seemed pretty dull after all that.

16

The Purple Horse

The purple horse may have been one of the most traveled stuffed creatures in memory. My memory anyway. I received him from some relative or family friend back in the 1940's. Probably around 1945. I have a vague memory of a matching red horse given to my little brother and he was born in 1944.

Purple stood about ten inches tall if you counted his ears which seemed to be made of some sort of oil cloth. His mane and tail looked like common kitchen string. Saddle and bridle were dark blue and printed on his purple hide. Still he had a jaunty, realistic air about him. His designer obviously had a good sense of 'horse.' No feel good fuzziness, no comic strip rendering.

The red horse wore out with my brother's rough boy ways and was discarded before long, but the purple horse held on. His first long journey was a car trip from Spearfish, South Dakota to Albany, Missouri. The poor beast rode in a box in the trunk of our ancient Chevy.

My dad had enrolled in a watch making school on the G.I. Bill when he was discharged from the Navy. My mom packed up a few things for our stay and us kids were told to pick one toy to take along. I chose the purple horse. The rest of our stuff went down the cellar steps to storage at my grandmother's house.

Me and that stuffed horse became well acquainted during those months in a cramped attic apartment. When our sentence was over, we hustled back to South Dakota. The purple horse rejoined his friends from Grandma's cellar and the whole troop of our belongings moved to temporary quarters in the Roundup Cabin Camp. The purple horse spent most of his time on the window sill of the upstairs bedroom, a bedroom shared by the four of us.

The following spring we moved into a real house where I had a dresser top to display my growing herd of horses, plastic, plaster, metal, and stuffed. The purple horse lost his status as the one and only.

In 1955 we packed up our stuff, loaded it in a trailer, and drove to Pasco, Washington. Like our canary the purple horse rode in the car. No packing box for him this trip, but the next few years were bumpy for both horse and owner. Junior high, high school, and a furry plush mouse from a boy friend pushed Old Purple into the background.

By the time I left home for college Purple's string tail was getting thin and his ears flopped over. He joined my other childish stuff in my mom's attic. Four years later my mom insisted I take my attic junk along when I moved to Alberta. That box stayed unopened in a closet until I hauled it back two years later. This time Old Purple was consigned to the rafters in the garage where he stayed for years and years listening to mice chewing on the doll clothes in the box next to him. A stronger box and a wad of tape kept Purple safe.

When the house was sold, my brother cleaned out the garage and hauled the boxes to Seattle. Surely they held something of value after all that time.

On a visit he brought the box along and dumped it in my living room. Your junk, he announced. The purple horse had returned. Along with a crew of battered dolls and rotting doll clothing. Not mine, I protested, but he refused to listen. I transferred the mess to a plastic box and shoved it up the ladder into the attic.

Now it is fifteen years later and the purple horse is nearly seventy years old. I haul the plastic box into my studio and unpack it. One pile for the trash, one for the doll club, one for the thrift shop, and the purple horse for me. The poor fellow looks like he had wallowed in a mud puddle these last years. It will take some careful cleaning to restore him. And some re-stitching and what about that tail. Can I figure out how to add a little string to it.

Somewhat cleaner, Old Purple stands on the shelf above my TV waiting for his next trip.

20

The Glass Horse Heads

December 1945 blustered in with a series of blizzards. Me and my mom had moved back home with Grandma and my youngest auntie who was due to graduate from High School in the spring. All of the Uncles were off in some fox hole somewhere. My dad was fixing ships for the Navy in San Diego. Rationing of just about everything dominated our lives. It was a wonder we even noticed Christmas coming.

My mom drove the winding hill road to her job at St. Joseph's Hospital in Deadwood night or day as her shift dictated. Auntie was elbow deep in books and term papers. Grandma was relegated to chief cook and washer woman. Everyone checked the post office for scarce letters from absent family.

Amid the worry and the work and the daily search for scarce items like sugar, gas, tires, suitable clothing, film, and coffee, we decided what we really needed was Christmas. We trekked up into the hills to cut a likely evergreen. Boxes of ornaments and tinsel from the attic transformed the wobbly little tree into Cinderella at the ball.

Whispered conversations meant that some effort to make or buy presents was going on. We sacrificed the last cup of hoarded sugar to make some rather odd cookies.

A trip to the five and dime provided an opportunity to buy presents. We couldn't find any wrapping paper or even cellophane tape so we used the glossy pages from old magazines. The newspaper, along with the Sears and Roebuck catalogue, had long been relegated to the status of toilet paper. A few old hair ribbons and a purloined roll of surgical tape served to hold things together.

For all our efforts the only thing I remember about that Christmas Day was the present Grandma and Auntie gave my mother. A pair of glass horse head bookends. Auntie had found them in the Deadwood five and dime on a school field trip. Pooling her money with Grandma's just covered the price.

I don't know how my mother felt about the clear glass horse heads, but I do know they moved with us over and over. From Spearfish they moved to Lead, South Dakota and from there to Albany, Missouri. From Albany they moved to the Roundup Cabin Camp in Belle Fourche, South Dakota and then to a house on Day Street. In 1955 the bookends made the trek in a trailer we pulled to Pasco, Washington. There they stayed until my brothers cleaned out the house after my parents died. They took the bookends to Seattle and later brought them to me in Port Angeles, Washington. Now they stand watching me write this. It is 2016.

Good as new and bright in the morning light, the glass horses gaze out at the Olympic Mountains. For the first time I wonder what they might be worth now. I pulled up a web site market place and typed in 'glass horse head bookends.' To my surprise twenty five or more sets, singles, and groups of three glass horse heads came up. Most of them looked exactly like mine. A few others were frosted glass and several had held the tiny bead-like candy so popular in the 1940's. I remembered a glass Scottie dog full of the bead candy I had received for my 7th birthday. The candy was awful but the glass dog had survived all these years. Maybe I should introduce the Scotty to the glass horses. Then I looked at the price of the bookends.

The price of the glass horse heads on the web site? $6.99 plus postage. $6.99 for a pristine antique more than seventy years old. The Scotty dog was priced a few dollars more.

I exited the web site and shut down the computer. Would I dust and polish mine less carefully next time or should I buy a couple of extra sets as backup in case mine were lost or damaged? Not all old things are antiques, no matter how beautiful or beloved they are.

The Journey of a Painting

Two Collies and a Canvas

In 1908 my grandmother, Hilma and her new husband, Charlie, homesteaded near Coal Springs, South Dakota. They came by train from Lincoln County as far as the railhead, then hired a wagon to take them and their house plunder to their claim. With hard work they had a sod house erected by the first snow fall.

One morning a young fellow appeared at their door. He held the reins of a thin brown horse in one hand, his hat in the other. He wondered if they had any work that needed doing. And could they direct him to cheap lodgings somewhere.

Hilma sized him up and ordered Charlie to take the horse to their lean-to stable and feed him while she dealt with the 'lad.' She soon had him seated at her table with a bowl of oat porridge and a mug of coffee.

She asked him what sort of work he wanted and where he was from and what brought him to this out of the way place. All the while she gave him a good looking over. He appeared to be a rancher's son with his store bought clothes and carved leather belt. His boots had a good polish on them and a chain at his pocket indicated a watch inside.

On the other hand he was rail thin, pale and tired looking with a wicked cough. His sandy hair and scruffy beard was way past needing a trip to the barber. A good scrubbing wouldn't hurt either.

'What can you do,' she asked him.' And how old are you?'
'You can call me Jake' he answered. 'Mostly I paint things.'
'Like barns and houses?'
'Well no. Like paintings you hang on your wall.'
'You're an artist?'

'I'd like to be. I see you have pictures on your wall.' He waved his hand in the direction of the framed prints that Hilma had on the wall of the soddy. 'I've never seen one of these shacks so prettied up.'

Hilma smiled and said she had first covered the dirt walls with blankets and material, then nailed the pictures up. She liked pictures.

Jake finished his breakfast and stood to examine the photos and art work more closely. 'I could paint you a nice picture. An original. It would look right nice here in the middle.'

'How much would that cost me?'

'Board and room for a few months,' said Jake. 'The doctor said I need a rest. Rest and fresh air. And besides winter is coming.'

Not one to ask many questions Hilma said she'd ask her husband. In the meantime he could put his bedroll in the corner by the door.

Jake spent the first few weeks scrounging up narrow bits of lumber to make his canvas frames. When he had a dozen or so frames made to his satisfaction, he hauled out a roll of raw canvas from his saddle bags and laid it out on the soddy floor. If his work in the cramped space aggravated the family, they didn't complain. With the canvas measured and cut Jake stretched a piece over the frame he had selected for Hilma's painting. Then he painted a layer of gray gook that looked like thick paint on the stretched canvas. The stink of it drove them from the soddy.

Charlie decided they needed to go to town about then and went to hitch up the buggy horse. They drove to nearby Coal Springs and bought flour, bacon, and a bottle of whiskey. Hilma added cough syrup, tea, and coffee to the order. There was little difference between the contents of the whiskey bottle and the cough medicine bottle.

When the three of them returned, the canvas had dried and the stink was mainly gone. Next time you do this, Jake, do it in the stable was Charlie's only comment.

The painting moved along rapidly and so did Jake's hacking cough. It seemed a race to see if he could finish the painting before the cough finished him. The cough syrup made him sleepy so Hilma only dosed him at bedtime.

Soon two collie dogs on a background of old Scotland sheep country emerged from Jake's paint brush. His brushwork was firm and sure for one so young and untaught. His golden brown dogs against the green countryside brought a promise of summer into the dark soddy during that long winter.

The only real indication of Jake's lack of art training was the difficulty he had with painting the dogs' far side eyes. He painted them and rubbed them out a dozen times before he gave up and moved on to the shading under the ears and the hint of sheep in the background.

Then as spring began to creep over the prairie, Jake declared the painting finished. Almost. Late one evening he climbed out of his bedroll and by the light of the glowing coals in the stove signed his name on the corner of the painting, then leaned it against the cupboard. By morning he was gone.

Hilma and Charlie lived in the sod house another three years before they moved into a regular house in town. By then they had three children. The collie painting moved with them. Many more moves and more children brought them to Spearfish, South Dakota. I remember the collie painting hanging in my grandmother's sitting room as early 1944 when I was three years old. Still unframed it had an old wad of string on the back to hitch over the nail in the wall. By the time I was in first grade the painting was mine. It hung, sometimes above the dresser in my room, other times on our living room wall in Belle Fourche.

In 1955 we moved to Pasco, Washington. A lot of our stuff was left behind. Childhood treasures like the big model airplane hanging in our dining room and the plaster hula girl won at the carnival. We found homes for our big yellow cat and a cocker puppy, but the collies and our one-eyed canary came with us. From 1955 to mid 1961 the collies hung in the living room. When I married in 1961 and went off to college, the collies were one of the first things I packed.

After three years at Washington State University we moved to Edmonton, Alberta. The collies followed in the moving van. Two years later they made the same sort of journey to southern Illinois. None of us liked the cold and frozen country of Alberta.

After a number of moves from one house to another we bought an isolated farm on the bank of the Big Muddy River and moved in. We unpacked boxes that had been sealed in Edmonton and once more the collies saw the light of day. They hung over the piano and supervised life at Nile Creek Farm for 28 years.

Then in 1998 we retired from the university, sold the farm, and prepared to move. I had spent months packing and sorting stuff. In addition to the usual household goods we had thousands upon thousands of books, a massive number of hand thrown pots made by my husband, and my own prints, drawings, and paintings. I culled like crazy until the local thrift shops locked their doors and pulled the shades when they saw me coming.

I did not cull the boxes of old photos and family items, but I did worry about consigning them to a box and placing them in the hands of an indifferent mover. Mostly I worried about the collies. They were getting old. Ninety years old. Though their paint was as bright as new, the wood stretcher frame and the canvas showed their age.

I finally sprung for a special box which the moving company said was made just for paintings. Also an insurance policy. The movers put our stuff in storage and we caught one of the last TWA flights to Seattle. From there we went on to Port Angeles and found a house on the banks of the Strait of Juan de Fuca.

Sometime in August we were united with our stuff and our cars. Except for the work of unpacking and settling in all was well.

The collies took their place on the counter of my studio good as new.

I had a new computer and something new—for me. An internet connection. One of the wonders of living in town along with garbage collection, a newspaper on our doorstep, and a single party phone line. TV too. We had been 28 years without such luxuries.

I decided it was time to research my family history and in the process found a web site for posts about Perkins County, South Dakota. Birth place to all of my aunts and uncles on my mother's side of the family. Also the collies.

At first I found little of interest and had no answering posts. Then several years later a fellow from Minnesota contacted me. He was from the very area where my grandparents had lived. I asked him about the name Jake had signed on the collie painting—J. L. Besler. He said he knew the family well and would pass the information about the painting along to them.

In February of 2013, around the collies' 105th birthday, a letter arrived from Fern Besler in Perkins County. She said Jake was her father-in-law's uncle. Jake had left home at a young age after a dispute with his father. Not so strange. Being an artist in that last frontier was a lot like writing left handed. Something to be corrected in those days.

After a few more letters and e-mails and a long conversation with the collies I said goodbye and sent them back to their homeland.

II. SPEARFISH

The Pony Ride

We lived in the middle of cow country surrounded by ranches with cattle and horses galore, yet we had never experienced either up close. We had had some precarious motorcycle rides hanging on to the back of a neighbor's nephew or grandson while he roared up and down the gravel alley behind our house. We had ridden in ancient automobiles as they huffed down main Street in the annual homecoming parade. We had stood on the back of tractors driven by older cousins and even made a short ride in an old biplane at the local airport, but never a horseback ride.

So when my Aunt Carol suggested rounding up the kids including me and my brother for a visit to the pony ride set up at City Park, she wasn't prepared for the chorus of 'no's' we voiced. She told us not to be such babies and herded us into her car. We punched each other and chanted baby, baby, baby all the way to the park. The youngest cousins were in tears when we finally climbed out of Auntie's car in the usually empty area across the road from the park.

A dozen or more horses and ponies were tied to the thin rail fence that outlined the riding ring. The dozing animals were saddled with their bridles hanging under their chins. Two teenage boys with forelocks much like the ponies they tended slouched near the sign advertising the rides. One boy collected the fee from Auntie, then lined us up from tallest on down to baby Jerry.

By the time he had us sorted the other boy had the bridles on the two biggest ponies. Me and my cousin, Lu, went first. The two boys hoisted us aboard the first two ponies. My helper jammed my feet into the stirrups and handed up the reins. A slap on the rump sent me and that spotted beast trundling onto the track that circled the inside of the rail fence. Lu's brown horse followed.

The other kids were mounted and sent into the circle behind us. The helper boys led the youngest cowboys who seemed unfazed by the whole thing. They urged the ponies to go faster, kicking and bouncing in their saddles.

After a couple of trips around the ring we relaxed a bit and tried to maneuver our mounts to veer right and left. Lu and I were marginally successful, but then cousin Jimmy and my brother tried whipping their ponies with the ends of the reins. My brother ended up flat on the ground with the pony standing over him. Jimmy and his pony took off down the road with the helpers racing to catch up. They soon discovered that very small horses run pretty fast.

One boy came back and mounted a bigger horse tied to the fence. He urged the horse into a gallop and disappeared down the road. The rest of us just gawked. When he returned he had Jimmy safe and sound in front of him in the saddle. In ten minutes or so the second helper walked in leading the runaway pony. They offered us a free ride to make up for the mess and bother, but we declined.

Fish and Fish Hooks

Rainbow Trout at Iron Creek

It was still dark when we loaded up the old Chevy with fishing gear and stuff for breakfast. In Spearfish we met up with my uncles. They had the boat and the beer. We drove up Tinton Road, past the Passion Play grounds on the old gravel road built by the WPA in the early 1930's. Iron Creek Lake lay about twelve miles farther into the Black Hills.

The men and boys of the WPA had also built the lake. A job that was finished in 1936. Years and years before that intrusion, a tribe of beavers had started the dam by falling trees across Iron Creek to make their homes. Legend has it that the beaver clan stood back and watched the workers strengthen and complete their century of work, then moved back in to bigger and better quarters on the shallow west side of the lake formed by the new dam.

It was still dark when we arrived at the lake. My dad and uncles went off to get the boat in the water, while the rest of us got a fire going. We had the coffee boiling and the bacon sizzling by the time they returned. The small boat waited for us at the dock. Eggs and bacon and boiled coffee tasted extra good in the fresh air, but we were baiting hooks by the time daylight arrived.

The mostly homemade boat held two adults and two children at most, so we took turns fishing from the dock. None of us knew how to swim and I doubt if we knew anything about life jackets either. At least we didn't have one.

The rainbow trout were biting like crazy and the adults soon had their limit. They turned their attention to teaching us kids how to fly cast. Maybe we would get our limit too and a huge orgy of fish eating would take place at Grandma's house in the evening.

The problem with fly casting is that hook sailing through the air. After tangling my line in the bushes behind me a second time, Uncle took the pole from me and demonstrated the cast again. Trouble was that he didn't always get it right either. The hook lost its worm and buried itself in my finger. The forward whip of the line set the hook just like it did in the fish's mouth.

I let out a bellow of surprise and pain. The grownups gathered around. One of them tried to work the hook out, but the barb made that impossible. Finally my dad got the side-cutters from his toolbox and snipped the end off the hook. That hurt, but it worked. Relieved, everyone went back to fishing, but I had had enough of fly casting. Ever.

We did have one whale of a good feast that evening.

Suckers on the Red Water

By the time my brother was toddling around my uncle started taking us fishing with him. Why? Who knows. One of the first of such excursions was to the Red Water River. About halfway between Spearfish and Belle Fourche the highway crossed the Red Water and made an easy access point for anyone dumb enough to want to fish the muddy river.

While Uncle fished vigorously and I dangled my line in the shallows, my brother made mud roads for his toy cars on the bank. We caught a stringer of the ugly smelly fish that lived under the bridge. We called them suckers because of the way their round mouths opened and closed nonstop.

Finally Uncle wore himself out baiting two hooks, pulling in those big lethargic fish, and making sure my brother stayed well away from both the water and the highway. He drove us home and presented my mother with our catch. Being a polite person, she kept a straight face until he drove out of the driveway.

We watched with open mouths when she offered the fish to our big yellow tom cat. The cat sniffed them and pawed one gingerly, then stuck his nose in the air and walked off. My mother buried the swatch of fish in the garden.

Orman Dam and the Monster Fish

Uncle's here, yelled my mom. Another fishing trip was in the offing. We choked down our breakfast and climbed into Uncle's car. New car we asked. Don't put your feet on the seat he answered.

We headed for Orman Dam. No trees, no soda pop, nothing but mud and stink. We were both car sick by the time Uncle turned off the main road. We bumped down the narrow track to the area at the edge of the main dam where he liked to fish.

The road into Orman Dam was dirt with deep ruts, but Uncle successfully steered up on the edge of the track to stay clear of the jutting ridge that had developed down the center. We lurched to a stop next to the trickle of water running through the shallow V in the face of the dam. When I got out of the car, the stench from the impounded water burned my eyes. What's wrong here Uncle? The Corps of Engineers are poisoning the lake, he said. To restock it.

We trudged to the end of the dam where it was easier to get to the water. The water level was low, so the big blocks on the inside face of the dam towered over us. It's a pretty tall dam, over a hundred feet tall. Of course that's out in the middle. Here on the end it's more like a two story building, about five cement blocks high.

While Uncle rigged his line he explained that he had to use a bigger sinker because the really huge fish were on the bottom where it was deep. The poison didn't kill them right away. It was just the little snots that bought the farm the first month or so. You could see them floating belly up farther out in the water.

I was very, very careful not to stand behind Uncle when he cast his line out into the lake. One time at Iron Creek he snagged me with a hook, run it right through my little finger. He and my dad finally cut the barbed end off with a side-cutter, so they could pull it out. Everybody said I ruined the whole fishing trip with my squalling because it scared away all the fish for two mile or more.

We tried fishing from the shore while Uncle in his hip boots worked the deep spots hunting a whopper. The margin of the lake was far too muddy to walk across without boots. I thought it was too far to cast the line from the dry shore.

My brother disagreed. He uncapped the tube that protected Uncle's extra rod and put the fragile sections together. He waved the rod around, barely missing the wall of the dam.

He found a jar of orangey-pink things the sporting goods store always sold for bait. They were round and slimy, packed in some clear yellow liquid. We carefully threaded a half-dozen on the hook.

Brother stood admiring his baited hook, sizing up the distance to the water. Now we need a weight, so I can cast this line past the mud to the water, he said. He found a flat, palm-sized whiskey bottle which he filled with dirt and tied to his line.

He walked out on the mud as far as he dared, as far as he could without breaking through the crust. With a fast look-see to be sure Uncle was engaged elsewhere, he pulled a length of line free of the reel, grabbed the line a couple of feet above the whiskey bottle sinker with his right hand, and whirled it around his head like a lasso. With a grunt he released the bottle. It sailed out over the mud to the deep water, trailing its hook loaded with nasty orange bait.

When the whiskey bottle hit the water, the springy rod bent almost double. I thought it would break, but it slowly straightened when Brother maneuvered more line from the reel. The concentric ring ripples spread out across the surface. For the space of about five deep breaths we were still, quiet, a sort of fishing tableaux, then all hell broke loose.

Whether Uncle saw the motion of Brother's cast out of the corner of his eye, or if the glint of sun on the whiskey bottle caught his attention, I don't know. He turned around in time to see the rod tip go under. In his hip waders he was at the scene instantly. I saw splashing, lots of splashing, then he broke through the mud crust and took a header right into the brackish gook.

Uncle reared up from the mud and hauled Brother and the fishing stuff to the shore. Get on back to the car, he told us, but we were too intent on watching the creature he had pulled across the mud with the fishing poles. Uncle was so busy knuckling his eyes and spitting mud, he hardly noticed the beast flopping around on the line we had baited with the slimy orange gobs. I tried to get his attention by jumping up and down and pointing, but he paid me no mind. By now the fish thing was doing back flips in the mud. I thought it might be his whopper, but it seemed small for a whopper. It was ugly, though. And it had whiskers, a whole face full of whiskers.

Brother scrambled up and grabbed the line attached to the fish. He must have stepped on the fishing rod, because I heard a loud snap. Got him, I got him. Get the net.

Don't touch it, roared Uncle. He was still rubbing sticky goo from his face, but he had finally noticed our fish. That old fish whipped those whiskers swish, wham, damn. Blood welled up across Brother's hand. That was the last time either of us got near one of those monsters.

We did get to go home then. All three of us sat on newspapers to preserve the upholstery in the Chevy, but there was nothing to be done about the stink of rotten fish that filled the air. Uncle Lester stopped the car in front of our house to let us out, but he didn't go in himself. It was a long time before we had to go fishing again.

Football Cold And Colder

On a late fall day my junior year in high school I accepted an invitation to a football game. A date actually. With a nice enough guy named Jim something or other who sat behind me in Spanish class. The Pasco High Bulldogs were having a winning streak for a change and even the non fans were paying attention. Hard not to with all the banners, pep rallies, and general rah, rah stuff going on. The halls were draped with white and purple crepe paper and in study hall the cheer leaders were allowed to come in and give us a couple of rambunctious cheers each morning.

Game night turned cold and snowy and I regretted accepting Jim's invitation. He didn't have a car and we were depending on his sister to drop us off at the stadium. I felt trapped already.

The game was tedious from the very beginning and Jim's amorous intentions surfaced by the end of the first quarter. He had brought a blanket and a flask of whiskey. That was warning enough. I shucked off the blanket and made an excuse to go down to the concessions. I tried to call my mom, but no one answered.

Damn it all. That left two choices. Submit to Jim's advances or walk home in the snow. I walked home. And remembered another football game long ago.

My folks, me, and my little brother lived in Belle Fourche, South Dakota. My aunt and her family lived in nearby Spearfish. We would drive the seven or eight miles to visit them after supper a few times a week. Usually the adults played cards, drank beer, and had a good old time for a few hours, then we would drive home. Everyone had to get up for work or school the next morning so it worked out okay.

One evening my uncle suggested we go to the Spearfish High School football game. They lived below the playing field on the edge of town. From their house you could hear the cheering for the Spartans when they made a good play. We decided to walk over.

The field was just that, a field with a few wooden bleachers along one side. No concessions, no shelter from wind, rain, or snow. A small shed to store equipment completed the complex.

For all the noise and bother there were very few spectators. We had our choice of seats. By the time we had spread out the blankets the snow was really bombing down. By the end of the first quarter we could barely see the players.

We draped the blankets over our heads and pulled scarves and jackets closer. The adults passed the whiskey bottle around and we made it to half time.

Chilled through and through we gave up and trudged back to my aunt's house. The snow was knee deep by the time we clomped onto the porch. We thumped most of the snow off each other before we went inside, but still made a wet soggy mess of Auntie's house.

After hot coffee and a good toweling off we were on our way home. So much for football.

Sledding, Sort Of

It was deep fall and my folks decided it was time to go deer hunting. The two mule deer they had bagged last year were long eaten and the locker at the freezer plant was nearly empty. A few packages of fat back, a couple of old hens, and a mystery package without a label. Not a good way to start winter.

They decided to make an expedition of it and called my mother's sister and her husband to ask them to join them. It was decided that we would drive to Auntie's house the day before and spend the night so as to get an early start the next morning.

None of us kids, brothers and cousins alike, were too enthused about the idea. We seldom saw each other and when we did it was like dogs and cats trapped in a big cardboard box. To stay overnight with the cousins was a tough sell, but meat on the table won out.

My mom sweetened the pot by telling us we could take our sleds and we scuttled off to load them in the car trunk. The snow was knee deep by now and the cousins lived on the edge of town with a big hill in back of their house.

Time to leave arrived. We piled into the car and were handed a casserole and a pitcher of iced tea to keep safe for the drive to Auntie's house. We would eat supper there as well as next morning's breakfast.

The cousins surveyed us warily when we pulled into their driveway, but managed to refrain from razzing us or throwing any rocks. Sometimes an adult presence was a good thing. Supper conversation was dominated by hunting talk that morphed into bragging about past hunts. The growing chorus of yawning from the rest of us finally penetrated the beer fogged brains of the adults. They suddenly realized that four in the morning was not far off.

We ended up in sleeping bags on the living room rug. The grownups got the beds. After a quick sleep and an even quicker breakfast and a wait for a turn in the bathroom everyone was dressed. Uncle went to fetch Grandma to look after us. We were zipped into our outside clothes and sent out to sled until the grownups were ready for the hunt. We could hear them arguing the merits of various weapons as we trooped out the door. Someone hollered at us to use the gentler west slope until it got daylight.

The snow on the hill was not as deep as we expected, but it was still a hard trudge to the top. We made a few tries at the west slope, but it had too many bare spots. We were ready to give it up and go back for breakfast, but the oldest of the cousins insisted we try the steeper south slope. We trudged up the hill again.

My cousin tried to get me to go first, but I needed to clean the gravelly sand out of my sled runners. We watched him shoot down the upper hill and disappear from sight. He whooped his arrival at the bottom and we prepared to join him.

I pushed off and nearly went airborne before I was quite settled. A series of twists and a pile of brush edged me closer to the rocky east side. I over corrected and shot across the path down the hill. Before I knew it I had crashed into a large boulder. Head first. That was enough sledding for me. I scrambled down the hill leaving my sled for the boys to retrieve and headed back to the house.

The adults paid little attention to my bleeding and pushed me in Grandma's direction. They were dressed, armed, and about to head to the woods. Whimpering children were not part of their plan. Grandma hauled me off to the bathroom and cleaned me up.

She told me it wasn't serious and stop blubbering. Felt serious to me though I don't know which hurt the most—my collision with the rock or the grownups ignoring me.

Around noon they came home with a couple of big black tail bucks draped over the car fenders, so that was some consolation. To me anyway. Not so good for the deer.

Fine Doings At Wildcat Cave

Wildcat Cave is hidden on a bluff just off the scenic highway south of Spearfish, South Dakota. Modern day hikers call it Community Cave for reasons very unclear to me. It probably irritates the wildcats too. Being displaced like that in the geography books and the internet.

I doubt if even the least cat would have any trouble handling the steep path from the creek bed, but it was and is a bit of a chore for us two legged cats. The trail is pretty much straight up and endowed with a few tons of loose rock.

Oddly enough I didn't notice these flaws in the trail the first time I went up there. Of course I was about five years old and still pretty close to the ground. My mom and her sisters and a couple of friends decided to picnic up there one day. My dad and various men friends were all away doing war time stuff so it was all women folk.

We parked on the pullout across from the trail. With much giggling the picnic basket and a couple of blankets were assembled on the car fender while two of the girls changed their shoes. Sneakers being more appropriate than the slick soled flats they usually wore.

We crossed the highway and slid down the bank to the creek. The creek was running fast, but only ankle deep. We hopped from rock to rock and missed getting wet altogether. We had a little trouble finding the first part of the trail in the tall grass and bushes, but after a couple of false starts we were on our way. After a scramble up a short stretch of trail, my aunties stopped for a breather. At least that's what they said. One of them pulled out a flask and took a swig, then passed it around. The giggling increased.

We clambered up the next section of the path, then had another breather. Or swig depending on how you interpreted it. The next section of trail was steeper and the aunties dislodged a lot of loose rock down on me and my mom. Mom joined the aunties swigging at the next stop.

With one last burst of effort we climbed through a mess of loose rock to find ourselves on level ground. It was dark and spooky there under the overhang of the cave roof. We could no longer hear the traffic noises from the highway. But when we turned around to face the canyon, the view was so beautiful.

Framed by the rough cave edges the million kinds of green with the sun shining through turned us to awed silence.

"Enough gawking," said one of the girls. "I'm starving." She turned her attention to unpacking the picnic and shaking out the blankets.

Unlike a closed in cave, Wildcat was narrowly long and open to the canyon for its entire length. It was dry and light until you walked to the back where a bunch of other caves with low openings lined the wall. Those openings seemed to breath cold moist air and an ominous hint of unseen beings. One of the girls said you could climb through one of the small caves to the overhanging bluff.

Which one? The question was discussed as we sat around eating our sandwiches.

"Someone should check. It would be fun to get up to the bluff top."

"Nuts to that. You'd have to crawl."

"And if you got the wrong one, you'd have to back out."

"Animals. Wild Cats. Probably living in there."

"I thought I saw eyes watching us. Glowing eyes."

"Small stuff here could check for us. Little enough to turn round in the cave." She looked right at me.

I launched myself into my mom's lap, squalling and up ending her coffee.

One of the girls looked over her shoulder toward the low caves and added her shrieks to mine. Yellow eyes in the darkness were watching us.

The picnic was over. The lunch basket was packed, the blankets wadded up. We scrambled back down the trail to the car.

Old Mining Towns: Carbonate 1

Our favorite Sunday recreation was hunting for a lost gold mining town called Carbonate. We lived in Belle Fourche, South Dakota, a cow town just north of the Black Hills. The hills held the remains of many old mines, wannabe gold mines, and plain old homesteads. Piles of hand hewn boards, rusty nails, slab sides from iron stoves, dim trails through the woods that had once been roads were everywhere if you had the eye for them.

In the 1880's there must have been a huge influx of people into the hills looking for their piece of the rainbow. Carbonate was a real town established by a man named James Ridpath. The first influx of about two hundred men lived in tents, drank from the stream, cooked over open fires, and crapped in the woods. When they got weary of such rudimentary living, a town grew quickly.

A wagon road wound down through the hills to Spearfish, but saloons, a reservoir, barber shop, restaurant, and a laundry grew on the mine site the summer of 1881. Even a newspaper. But the mine produced carbonate ore which is a mix of silver and lead rather than the much sought gold of other mines, most notably the Homestake Mine in nearby Lead. By 1883 the mine closed and the town faded. It got going again in 1885 along with a half dozen other mines in the area when gold was discovered nearby. This time the town gained a church, a school, a bank, and several gambling halls. Also a cemetery. By 1891 the mine turned a profit of nearly $700,000.

By 1889 the cemetery was also booming. Diphtheria epidemics and bad living conditions ravaged the population over the next few years. Fumes from the smelter killed the town cats and spared the rats which carried numerous diseases. The fumes probably didn't do the human element any good either. Carbonate was doomed along with its many counterparts scattered throughout the hills.

It was these dim remains that we searched for each Sunday. The roads had pretty much disappeared, grown up in trees and poison ivy. Hunters had kept a few of them passable, but usually we drove as far as we could and then hiked what little of the path we could make out. Sometimes we got lucky and found the road again after crossing a tangled area.

One fine day we stumbled across the bed of a narrow gauge railroad. My dad examined the terrain and decided he could get the car through the rough patch so he left us there and went back for the car. He had an unerring sense of direction and returned, with the car, about 45 minutes later. We spread our lunch on the rail bed and ate. Then we took off driving down the super highway of the past.

After a few miles the forest gave way to a huge meadow. There we found the crumbled remains of half dozen log buildings, one room cabins, none of them more than twelve foot square. One or two had windows, the others were dark cubes. Hand hewn shingles that had once repelled the rain and snow lay in heaps along with shattered glass and trash. Rags and papers were piled in the corners of the biggest structure.

Paper. We had never found paper in any of our searches. It must have been the mine office. The remains of pigeon hole mail slots leaned against one wall and a counter stood on unsteady legs.

We found an unused pile of requisition forms tattered and rat chewed, then a time card half filled in. The form was titled 'New reliance Gold Mining Co.' The name 'Morton' was printed across the top and it was dated 5/28/13. 1913. Unfortunately the company name did not match with what we knew about Carbonate. Still the place was a treasure to us.

In a dark protected corner of one of the cabins I found an old catalogue advertising saddles, harness, and other such gear. It was dated 1923. This mine site was much newer than Carbonate. My dad agreed.

The terrain wasn't right either. Carbonate had sat in a large clearing, but the mine itself was said to be in the side of a large steep hill above a canyon. No hills, no canyon here.

My dad warned us about the open areas around the cabins. They could be treacherous. Old cisterns and dry shafts were everywhere. Other holes were attempts at well digging. Mounds and pits dotted the area around the cabins and the ground could give way without notice. A disquieting thought. We could plunge clear to China with a misplaced step.

My brother and I decided to stick to the piles of rubbish and leave the outlying exploration to the adults. We were struggling to lift an elaborate cast iron stove door into the trunk when my dad came back to tell us he had found an easier way out of the woods. A real road. Nice we said, now can you help us with our treasure.

My dad hoisted the cast iron thing into the trunk with ease. An interesting design he said. Pretty fancy for a mining camp.

The oval door was cast in a pattern of Greek columns with a face in the center. An enameled blue medallion shaped like a flower topped the door. A few minutes later we found the back panel of the stove with the same design but no blue flower. Why do the doors have legs we asked.

We later learned that the two panels fit either end of a barrel to make a fairly large stove. For us they became lawn ornaments.

There was a chill in the air by the time we got the stove parts loaded into the trunk and headed out of the woods to the main road to Lead. A good day of hunting we thought. The stove, my old catalogue, a sample of the papers from the mine office. My dad said maybe we would find Carbonate another weekend.

Carbonate 2

Sunday morning and we were getting ready for an excursion into the Black Hills to search for old towns, mines, and homesteads. We were just poking around said my dad, but it wouldn't hurt if we found Carbonate while we were at it.

It was a beautiful summer day. Calm and clear. We had made a big pot of chili the night before and it radiated tongue lolling rays as my mother lowered it into a cardboard box. Wrapped in several layers of towel, the chili in its heavy aluminum pot would still be hot hours later. Bowls, spoons, paper napkins, and crackers went in another box. We would pick up a few bottles of pop at the Sinclair station on the way out of town.

I guess my dad had another lead on the location of Carbonate. Probably some story one of his customers at Smith's Jewelry store told him. We were underway by ten in the morning after about three trips each to the bathroom.

A few miles south of Spearfish on the canyon road we slowed and turned onto a dirt road. One with big rocks poking out of it. The road went across Spearfish Creek and came out at a small lodge with several cabins you could rent. We drove across the parking lot and found a dim set of tracks on the other side. We bumped down this almost road for another mile or so before we had to stop. Too many fallen trees in the road.

We decided to continue and left the car in our wake. Very quickly the road steepened and turned into a narrow path along the side of the mountain. Straight up on the left, straight down on the right. No turning back now, said my dad, so we picked our way across the shale laced face of the slope to the forest on the other side.

How are we gonna get back asked my brother as we stood looking at the way we had come. Probably an easier way said my dad. Don't worry about it. The path plunged into the trees and we plunged after it. The narrow valley soon widened into a grassy field. A few hewn boards lay here and there. Some were propped against the scattered trees. Closer inspection revealed carved names and dates. A cemetery said my mom. We're standing in a graveyard.

A very old one because what little we could make out of the dates started with 18. Too spooky so we kept moving. A few heaps that had been cabins were next. Nothing had survived here. Beams, siding, roofing had all become compost. Then we looked up.

The remains of the mine towered far above us on the cliff edge. The collapsed shaft entrance looked like the mouth of some weird monster with the remains of narrow gauge rails curling out of it. An old ore cart hung off the edge above our heads. One of its wheels looked like it could crush the whole lot of us. Other rusting equipment peered through the underbrush above the mine shaft. A triangle lift of some sort towered over a ruined structure straddling the mine entrance. It must have been built of store bought timbers to have lasted this long, said my dad, creosoted probably.

We backed away from the rusted mess hulking above our heads. After poking through a few more grass covered mounds we decided there was little of interest at this site. My dad climbed up to the mine entrance to see if he could find anything to identify the place, but returned empty handed.

My mom thought we should look more closely at the cemetery. Since we had to go through it to get back to the car, we obliged by looking through the ruined grave markers with care. We copied down the few bits of names and dates we found. Maybe someone could figure out the puzzle.

Our hopes for an easier route back to civilization did not pan out and we had a slow hike back across the mountain face. We were growling with hunger by the time we made it back to the car. The pot of chili and warm soda pop more than made up for a disappointing day of exploring.

III. Belle Fourche: The Beautiful Forks

The Big Snow

When we woke up on January 2nd it was oddly dark. The days had been getting longer and the second of January was a Sunday so we were sleeping in, but it was still dark. When my dad went to get the newspaper all was revealed.

"Snowed last night. Come see."

"Do we have to? It's cold."

I snickered down under the covers to warm my nose, but the summons became more insistent. My brother finally detached from his warm bed and pulled my blankets to the floor as he ran by.

"Look, kiddos." My dad opened the inner door to reveal the glass of the storm door showing solid snow, clear to the roof. We ran from room to room, but the story was the same—snow as far up as we could see, covering every door and window.

The power was off, but we had gas for heat and cooking so Mom went about whipping up breakfast. Somewhere around the second slice of raisin bread toast the phone rang. Trouble, it was always trouble when that thing rang. We could hear Mom's end of the conversation clearly along with scraps of the caller's dialogue.

"But it's my two days off. I just worked the night shift."

"..so sorry...no one else..."

"We are totally snowed in here."

"..women in labor...accident victims...heart attack..."

"I'm sorry. Can't you call one of the others? How about Chase? Or Hanson?"

"..out in the country...snow is worse..."

"If I can't, I can't. We are snowed in here solid."

"..get ready..come for you..."

My dad took the phone and tried to explain the situation in a firmer tone, but to no avail. He hung up with a parting promise to start shoveling a path to the street.

"Best get ready, Ma. They are coming to pick you up. Better pack an overnight bag."

He left the room to change into his outdoor clothes. He came back with a screwdriver and a shovel and began removing the glass section of the storm door. By the time he had shoveled his way out of the house my mom was dressed in her white uniform.

She stood patting her hair into place before pinning her starched nurses cap in place. The seams in her white nylons were perfectly straight and her navy blue pea coat lay on the arm of the couch waiting along with her overnight bag.

"You kiddos going to be good now? Take care of your papa and help out."

"Listen. Sirens. I hear sirens," I said.

"Where? Where?" My brother ran to the window, but it was still snow covered of course. Dummy. Lighter maybe, but still covered.

"Get your snow suits and you can go out."

As my dad shoveled, the sirens became louder and louder. We crawled out the opening in the storm door and climbed the huge mound of snow to see what was going on. It was like a desert of snow as far as the horizon.

"The sirens are coming from across the river," said my brother.

"I can't see anything."

"Look close. On the bridge approach. The snow must not be as deep there."

"Red lights."

By the time my dad's shoveled path reached the street, we could see the county road grader chewing its way up our street. It threw great clouds of snow on either side but left a smooth path behind. Harry Hantz, the town's police chief, followed with all his lights and sirens going full blast. While he maneuvered to turn around in the narrow space, my dad came back to the house to escort Mom to the street. The road grader plowed to the next house, then turned around to lead the police car back across town to the hospital.

Later the neighbors grumbled about their unplowed streets, but we had a few days of feeling superior. My mom had three hard days at the hospital before she came home.

54

Apendictionary Or Pendicitus Or Whatever

My Operation at John Burns Hospital

Operation! Hospital! Good grief, can this make interesting reading, or writing for that matter? Guess we will find out.

In September of 1947 we moved to Belle Fourche, South Dakota. We couldn't find a house to buy or rent so we moved into the Roundup Cabin Camp which leased its tourist cabins for the nine month off season. It was an okay place to live, at least in my mind. Nice steep stairs for sliding down, a bed jammed into the same room as my parents and baby brother, a lot of grassy play place, and a rushing stream out back. The cabins, government surplus grain elevators, sat in a big circle around a gravel drive with all sorts of odd people living in them.

I was six years old and hadn't started school yet. The adults were too busy with new jobs and moving to think of such trivial things. I didn't remind them.

One morning I woke up feeling worse than awful. I could hear voices downstairs so I knew it was time to get up. I struggled into my jeans and had one arm poked into my flannel shirt when I had an overwhelming need to throw up. I slid down the stairs on my butt and staggered into the bathroom. My mom followed and held my forehead with one hand and my tummy with the other as I puked into the sink.

Wrapped in a blanket they hustled me out to the car and drove to the hospital. Not much trouble, so far, because my mom was a nurse there and was on her way to work her shift. My dad dropped us off and went to work.

A nurse came and led us to an exam room where someone stuck my finger and squeezed out a big dollop of blood. It was a momentary distraction. By now I was heaving out one end and pooping out the other.

Next thing I remember was a doctor type guy trying to hold a rubber gadget over my face. Count, he commanded. By the time I figured that out I had spiraled out into oblivion. The next thing I remember was waking up cold, so very cold, more than snow bank cold. A nurse brought a heated blanket, but to no avail. Surely I was turning blue.

My mom appeared and yanked the bed clothes off. I could only whimper. Get the doctor, she commanded. She's bleeding. Actually she said hemorrhaging, but I didn't learn that word until years later.

The doctor that arrived was not the gruff old guy that had demanded I count when all I wanted to do was puke. This one was young and he smiled at me. Fix you up in a jiffy, he said and winked.

They wheeled my bed out into the hallway. Wouldn't want to frighten the other young lady, he said. I hadn't even noticed I had a roommate which was pretty odd considering the loud crying and whimpering coming from her corner of the room.

A huge light with a reflector behind it was wheeled into the dark hallway. While the nurses assembled an array of instruments, my doctor guy washed up and squeezed his big hands into rubber gloves. He selected a bandage scissors from the tray on a wheeled cart. I knew they were bandage scissors because my mom had brought home a pair which I used to cut out paper dolls.

He had a nurse crank up the head of the bed so I could watch him snip through the humongous bandage wrapped around my middle. He slipped the blood soaked mess away from my still numb skin and a nurse dropped it into the trash. Pretty yucky, he commented, don't you think?

Blood was oozing everywhere when he snipped through the sutures. Must be inside because this stitching is quite perfect, he muttered. He asked the nurse to bring something with an unpronounceable name and waited while she unwrapped a package of white stuff.

With a tool that looked like something for serving salad he plucked a white cube from the package. He held it up for my inspection. Looks like a big sugar lump doesn't it. Works like magic though.

He proceeded to pack me full of those white cubes. As he worked I started warming up and I was sound asleep by the time he finished. Even the crying girl in the corner bed could not penetrate my brain. So much for appendectomies.

58

Two Montana Cousins

It was a fine June day when my dad got a phone call from his older brother in Whitefish, Montana. There was a lot of wrangling back and forth and our normally quiet Father was shouting when he slammed the phone down.

"Art's two boys will be on the evening bus," he told my mom. "He expects me to find them summer work. And put them up too."

"I guess they can sleep on the rollaway. You haven't seen Art in twenty years have you?"

"More like ten or twelve. Those boys were small then. How can he do this?"

The two strangers that stomped into our kitchen late that Saturday night seemed huge and very loud to me. They didn't speak to us, but jostled and punched each other. My dad said that the bus had been delayed in Ekalaka with a flat tire.

Mom showed them where they were to sleep and gave them a turn in the bathroom before she turned off the lights. We could hear the rollaway in the living room creak in time with loud snores off and on all night.

Attempts at fitting these strangers into our schedule seemed doomed to failure from the beginning. They were up and out of the house before breakfast doing what we did not know. They returned at ten o'clock expecting to be fed. Mom told them they had to wait until lunch time. They settled down on the living room rug to play penny ante or something.

"Wonder why Art thought there would be any work around here," said my mom. "Did you ask around."

"May be something at the blacksmith shop. I'll take them down to see Ray on Monday."

Ray said he'd give the older cousin a try. Whitefish cousin spent the week sorting and stacking pieces of junked cars and trying to bend his mind around the idea of taking orders from a boss. The younger one sat on the sidewalk outside and caged cigarettes. Saturday was payday and the cousins did not show up for supper. At ten we gave up waiting for them to appear, turned off the lights, and went to bed.

Around two in the morning they staggered in, soused to the gills. My dad ordered us to stay in bed. He'd deal with them. It was a long night and we were a grumpy bunch in the morning.

Mom demanded that the cousins clean up the mess they had made on their early morning return before she would feed them. Ever again. The house reeked. Apparently they had puked all over the living room on their return. My dad threatened them with slow death if they didn't tell him where they got the booze. Neither happened.

Later that day of disruption my dad put them to painting our picket fence. That lasted about an hour before the two boys tried to dodge the work by brow beating me and my brother into doing it. That earned them a good dose of my dad's temper. Their next ploy was doing the job as poorly as possible and boy were they good at being bad. Paint everywhere except on the fence. How had Ray managed to put up with such behavior for a whole week was beyond me.

About an hour later my dad appeared with the boys' stuff. One duffle bag in each hand with their crap spilling out. He ordered the cousins into the car. He ignored the shocked looks on their faces and dumped the bags into the trunk and returned to stand waiting with his arms crossed. The younger cousin climbed into the back seat leaving a smear of paint on the car door. The older one spat a couple of times then followed suit.

When my dad got back from the bus station he washed the car, then came in and took a shower. It took my mom considerably longer to get the living room shipshape. She burned the sheets and got the rollaway hauled to the dump. Case closed.

We never heard from the Whitefish branch of the family again. At least not for another ten years.

62

The Buckskin Mare and the Pole Corral

Back in the early 1950's our town had probably never heard of zoning regulations, permits, building codes, and licenses for this, that and everything. Belle Fourche was a tiny community in Western South Dakota.

We did have dog licenses, but no dog catcher. If you wanted a drivers permit, all it required was a trip to the court house and fifty cents. You didn't even need to be able to see as one blind resident proved. He flashed his driver's license around at every opportunity.

Our house sat on a quarter of a city lot as did the house to the north of us. Another house in the next block was built across a city alley and smack on the edge of the street. Just up our alley was a house with a barn and a pole corral. The corral poles were set as close to the alley as possible. They rattled in their wire hangers with each passing car or truck. So much for easements.

That place was owned by a local rancher. He had many acres of prairie land some forty miles away, but lived in town so his daughter could go to high school and take part in all the high school stuff.

One beast or another lived in his barn and its attached corral for a few days or months year around. Usually it was a horse or two or a mule, but donkeys and Hereford cows also lived there at times. The mares had been brought in from the range as foaling time approached. The roping horses were mostly in need of treatment for various cuts, scrapes, and sprains.

Some animals arrived on sale day. Some to go through the sales ring, others had been bought and were on their way to the ranch. Once there was even a shaggy camel on his way to the Passion Play in nearby Spearfish.

Daily, I would sneak the time to trek up the alley to visit the animals in the corral. Much more interesting than the fourteen cent movies or listening to the Lone Ranger on the radio. I even managed to skip on some homework every now and then.

One summer day I arrived in time to see a horse being unloaded into the corral. The buckskin mare had tried to kick her way out of the trailer and managed to get wedged in sideways. A couple of cowboys grabbed her tail and got her turned around and out of the trailer. She bucked and snorted and carried on something terrible, but she was a beauty with long black mane and tail.

I did my best to befriend the mare. She rolled her eyes and spurned my offers of sugar lumps and newly cut grass. After a few visits she would race across the corral towards me. She would slide to a stop inches from the fence with her ears back and teeth showing. Shaking and sweating she would stand and glare at me until I turned tail and ran home.

Every day for a week we repeated this ritual, then it escalated. On a particularly hot day the mare whirled and lashed out with her heels. She caught the top rail of the fence and sent it crashing to the dirt. That brought the owner out to investigate. He said nothing. Just lifted the fence rail back in place and disappeared into the house.

For a few days I gave my attempts to befriend the mare a rest. I had a ton of homework and besides it was raining. I did wonder why she was here in town. She wasn't about to foal and she had no obvious injuries that needed tending.

The next time I saw her she was really feeling her oats. Bucking and squealing and showing her heels to a small crowd of neighbors. Her reputation had spread. Probably because of the racket she made kicking the side of the barn and squealing at everything that walked past the corral. What earthly good could this creature be?

Later that day I returned to the corral with a bucket of sweet feed I had begged from another neighbor. Head down, one foot cocked, the mare stood facing away from me. Maybe she was napping for a change. Squatting down next to the fence I poured the sweet treat out on the ground in a mound.

Quick as lightening her head snapped up and she whirled around. I swear she had all four feet off the ground. When she reached the fence she barely slowed down. Fence poles flew everywhere. Thoughts of sudden death suddenly crossed my mind. The noise of the fence crashing to the ground saved me. The mare snorted and kicked, then whirled back around and retreated to the barn. Someone slammed the door shut and I took off for home.

I ended up getting grounded for a month. The mare's intended owner showed up a few days later. He was a stock contractor buying bucking stock for the rodeo circuit.

Revenge for the Stinky Car

My mom and dad along with Auntie Carol and her kid, Jimmie, were going fishing at the beaver dams up off the road to Iron Creek. Before dawn we loaded the old Chevy with fishing gear, a can filled with dirt and worms and another one with coffee. A cast iron frying pan, bacon, and a carton of eggs, a loaf of Bunny bread, paper plates, forks, and coffee mugs crammed into the box with the coffee and worms.

We bumped up the dirt road until we were at about the halfway point from Spearfish to Iron Creek. My dad stopped the car and we jumped out to be sure the dim track leading off into the woods was, indeed, the way to the beaver dams. After a bit of sleepy argument it was decided that we were at the right turnoff.

My mom and auntie opened the barb wire gate and my dad drove into the ditch and up the other side on this so-called road. The ladies, my dad called them 'the girls,' fastened the gate behind us.

A mile or so farther on the track opened onto a large meadow with a series of lazy ponds built by the beavers. Our secret fishing hole.

In the almost light of the new day we gathered sticks and a half rotted section of log for our breakfast fire. Soon we had water boiling and the bacon frying. Coffee added to the boiling water made a heavy brew whose perfume vied with the forest scent of pine and spruce and the smoke from our fire. When the bacon was brown and crisp, it was forked out of the pan. Bacon out, the eggs went in. Next my dad drained the grease and added the bread to the hot pan. Our almost toast.

We sat on a fallen tree and ate. In the cold woodsy morning it seemed a feast. Jimmy, who was still pretty much a baby, had a bottle of formula and a few spoons of pre-cooked cereal. After breakfast the adults wandered off to wrestle with the fishing gear and find a good spot for fly casting. I got stuck with watching Jimmy. Mostly not letting him near the water.

Auntie came back once to change his diaper and pour herself another cup of the campfire coffee. She offered me a half cup, but the muddy brew had lost its mystique. After a couple of sips I dumped it in the bushes.

By noon the fish had ceased biting. We gathered up our stuff, dumped the trash behind a tree, and climbed into the car for the trip home. It was a fairly typical fishing trip for us.

Over the next few weeks my mom complained that the car had developed a nasty smell. My dad walked to work so he didn't pay much attention to her until he drove us to nearby Spearfish to visit Grandma. About the time we reached the Sinclair station on the outskirts of town the car got pretty ripe. By the time we pulled into Grandma's driveway we had all the windows down. While we went in the house, he made a cursory examination of the car, but reported he had found nothing out of order.

When we drove home, we went slowly at first to see if that had any effect on the smell. When it didn't, we drove very fast to get it over with as soon as possible.

The following Sunday my dad had all but dismantled the car looking for the problem. He was good with car problems and repairs, but this was outside his area of expertise. No car in its right mind could stink like this.

After work on Monday my dad made another go at the car stink mystery. This time he focused on the trunk which seemed to be the center of the problem. The weather had heated up considerably and the car didn't need to be driven to start the stink. First he pulled out all of the tools and stuff needed to keep the old heap running. Next came the spare tire which was held secure in a kind of holder against the right hand side of the trunk wall.

A slit had been made in the fabric covering the interior of the trunk to reach a solid place to fasten the tire bracket. My dad pulled the fabric aside and felt around, then he yelled for my mom. 'This,' he shouted, 'this is the stink.' He dropped a stinking wad at her feet and ran for the house to wash his hands.

The wad proved to be a very full cloth diaper long past its recyclable date. My mom found a shovel and scooped the mess into the trash. 'Damn that sister. Never, never let her near our car again.'

The next few weeks we plotted our revenge. It had to be spectacular and cause a lot of trouble, but no real harm. Something memorable for sure. As the plan developed we made a visit to the Army surplus store in Sturgis. There we found an old weather balloon leftover from some secret project in the dim past. My dad asked if the balloon still held air and was told it was good a new. Maybe never used even. For ten bucks we had our secret weapon.

We stowed the balloon and the air pump in the newly freshened trunk of our car and waited our chance, an evening when we knew Auntie and her family would be out of town.

Getting into the house was a cinch since no one locked their doors. We carefully moved lamps, ash trays, and toys to a back bedroom while my dad set up the balloon in the middle of the living room. We took turns pumping and soon had the balloon thumping the edges of the room.

We retreated to the front door and kept pumping. By peering in the windows we could watch the balloon move into the dining room and kitchen. By the time it touched the living room ceiling it had also filled the hallway to the back door. We put in another ten minutes of pumping to make sure the balloon was as full as we could possibly get it.

Exhausted, but gleeful, we piled into the car and drove home.

Coming 'Round The Mountain

When my cousin Lu suggested I team up with a couple of my girl friends and enter the spring talent show at school, I was floored. Talent, that meant singing and dancing and music making of various sorts. I didn't care much for any of those things. Horses, shooting marbles, and reading stacks of books was more my line.

Lu said, nonsense, and called two of the girls in my fourth grade class. Linda and Marlys were thrilled to join our 'group' and have a real life expert to teach us the tricks for a winning act.

My cousin, Lu, who lived in Pasco, Washington had won several beauty pageants and dance competitions in her senior year and the following summer. She had even gone to Hollywood with her dance group to compete.

Unfortunately choosing husbands wasn't one of her talents.

Marriage soon after her Hollywood trip proved to be her undoing. Her beloved turned out to be a drunk and an abuser and Lu ran home to Daddy as quick as her long, shapely legs could carry her. Her parents sent her to South Dakota to live with us for a few months while Daddy got her marriage annulled and the irate ex subdued.

So the spring of 1952 was a strange time for our household with our high maintenance cousin sleeping on the rollaway in the living room. She ate the leftovers Mom saved for supper and played the record player too late and too loud. My dad finally removed the needle and that stopped the music. There wasn't much defense for the rest of her high class ways, so we just ignored them.

But now we had the music back and under the direction of Cousin Lu my friends and I were doing the Bunny Hop until the floor shook. At least we thought that's what we were doing. Lu wasn't impressed. She was pretty sure we didn't know our left foot from the right and our elbows stuck out too much. And collapsing in a heap of giggles was not in the script.

Time for a change of direction. We would try singing. Ballads and opera were out. We had little vocal range, a highfalutin word for 'geez, kids. You can't sing.' We finally settled on the less demanding 'She'll Be Coming 'Round the Mountain When She Comes.'

Pleased with our ability to make difficult decisions, we took a break and went to the movies. Lu suffered through the first fifteen minutes of the oat burner, then whispered that she would be in the hotel café across the street when we finished with 'this nonsense.'

We finally got on with the business of polishing up our entry in the talent show. Every night after school we learned another verse and added our own touches. The verse that began with 'She'll be wearing red pajamas' was vetoed by the adults as being too suggestive. Whatever that meant. We argued about emphasis and costumes, but got on fairly well. Even Lu seemed mollified by our willing hard work.

When we told our teacher about our song, she told us it was an old, old church song that referred to the Second Coming of Christ and the Rapture. Being lapsed Lutherans, we had no idea what she was talking about, but thanked her politely.

She elaborated by telling us it was a simple 'call and response' song written in the 1800's. She sang a few verses to demonstrate.

King Jesus, he'll be driver, when she [the Rapture] comes...
She'll be loaded with bright angels, when she comes...
She will neither rock nor totter, when she comes...
She will run so level and steady, when she comes...
She will take us to the portals, when she comes...

As the song spread from Appalachia, the words changed to the familiar children's version that Lu was trying to teach us dummies.

After school we continued to wail our way through 'driving six white horses, when she comes,' 'we'll all come out to meet her when she comes,' and 'kill the old red rooster when she comes.' It was a hoot. After a week of practice we were planning our costumes.

Straw hats, checkered shirts, and blue jeans. What could be easier? When we showed up back stage on the night of our performance, we were directed to one of the classrooms for makeup. Makeup? What? Nobody told us about that. Lu was sitting in the audience with my parents and brothers, so she was no help. We were on our own.

We trooped into the makeup room and suffered the indignity of several sets of helping hands shuffling us through the process of being made stage ready. Powder, lipstick, dots of eye makeup on our cheeks to resemble freckles. When we complained it looked goofy, we were told we had to show up under bright lights. And the audience was a long way away.

We were told to give our music to the piano lady, then wait our turn. At least Lu had warned us about this detail and we gave the piano lady the page we had torn out of our song book. Now it was just the waiting for the endless line of acts ahead of us. Linda needed to pee, but held it like a trooper so we wouldn't lose our place in line.

When our names were announced, we stumbled on stage. Boy, were they ever right about the lights being bright. We could barely see. When our music started, it took us a ridiculous number of seconds to recognize it and launch into our song. At least we couldn't see the audience through the glare.

We sang like crazy and added in a few steps of the bunny hop for good measure. Down home hillbilly girls at their finest. By the end of our number our hair was undone and our lipstick smeared every which way, but the audience applauded with vigor. We were a success.

Backstage we were trying to remove the layers of makeup when the principle began announcing the winners. It had never actually occurred to us that we might have a chance of winning anything. We may not have even known there was any judging going on.

We edged back into the auditorium with our fellow singers and dancers to listen to the list of winners. With the stage lights turned down we could see out into the audience.

While we waited, the huge turnout of folks dawned on us. Folding chairs had been brought out for the overflow crowd and a number of people were standing across the back of the auditorium.

When the principle announced the winner of the vocal division we applauded the sixth grade boy named Stanley who had poured his heart and a great deal of talent into singing 'A Little White Cloud.' Dressed to the nines in a black suit and red bow tie, he walked on stage to take a bow.

Total shock about knocked us down when we were announced as the second place winners. Prodded by a teacher, we trooped out onto the stage elbowing each other and trying not to be first. The audience roared and stood up to applaud.

Life is strange. We never did that again. Stanley, however sang his way through college and became a music teacher at a well known school. Cousin Lu went home and found a nice fellow to marry for real. And me? Well I'm writing this so that should count for something.

Those Salad Eating Brownie Scouts

Third grade happened in an ancient brick building across the street from the United Methodist Church. The Brownie Scouts met in the basement of the church. My mom decided I needed to broaden my horizons and meet some nice girls. Get away from the troop of rowdy boys that populated our neighborhood. Get the picture?

The wave of noise that hit me the first time I walked down those basement steps almost sunk her program for me. If Mom hadn't had a firm grip on my hand, I would have bolted and never looked back. She decided she needed to stick around and signed up to be a helper. I was roped and hog tied. No escape.

The first few meetings were almost okay. We made plaster of Paris patties and pressed our hand prints into them. A hole and a hanging ribbon and you had an enormously heavy Christmas tree ornament. I still have mine. Another project involved cooking. No problem there. Knitting, or maybe it was crocheting, netted me some rough handed criticism. Too tight and lumpy. Likewise sewing. I mostly stuck myself with the needle. A lot.

I can't remember any of the girls I was supposed to befriend, but I do remember an outing to a camp on the edge of the Black Hills. A timber lodge and a parking lot deep in the forest. We were not permitted in the lodge and had to use the privy out in the trees. We were directed to a hand pump behind the lodge for water. The only bright spot was the fact that my mom had only signed us up for a day trip. Most of the other girls were pitching tents for a weekend stay.

Picnic baskets were hauled from the dozen or so cars in the parking lot and lugged to the tables. Checked oil cloths covered the gunk of centuries embedded in the weathered wood. Each of us had an assigned job as various bags, bottles, and bowls of food and drink were laid out. It didn't take long for every bug within ten miles discover our presence. Between swatting and scratching I was instructed in the fine art of salad making.

Salad. I had never heard of such a thing. We got our veggies from a can. Mostly pale green beans, peas, and soggy corn, though we did have roasting ears when we got up the gumption to make a raid on one of the small plots of field corn growing on the edge of the hills. Stealing I guess.

The scout leader helper plunked a huge plastic bowl down in front of me. Next came green stuff she called 'roman' or something, tomatoes, an onion, and two or three flabby peppers. I asked if the ground black stuff we sprinkled on boiled potatoes came from those lumpy things. She laughed at me and said wash the tomatoes and peppers. In what? Cold water in a bucket. My disgust level rose another notch.

With a lot of cutting and chopping we finally had salad assembled in the bowl. While the leader lady scrambled the ingredients together, I went to toss the scraps in the woods. By the time I wandered back the girls were lining up to fill their plates. I fell in behind a fourth grader several feet taller than me and shuffled along the row of tables.

Cold fried chicken. Check. Potato salad. Check. Red Jell-o with fruit cocktail. Check. Then came trouble. The scout lady shoveled a heap of salad onto my plate and poured some ugly oily orange gunk over it. I almost dropped my plate. It's French dressing she told me. Grossed out, I carried my plate to a nearby table and launched a rescue mission to save my lunch from the rivers of invading dressing.

I was about to toss the offending tomato slices into the grass, when the head Brownie lady appeared. She announced that the scout rule is you have to taste everything on your plate. Put that raw infected tomato in my mouth? Are you kidding? I had never eaten a raw tomato in my life. In my world tomatoes came scrunched to a pulp in a can. Are these things even edible? Even the pilgrims thought tomatoes were poison.

Not appropriate behavior for scout, she said. About the time she hauled me off the bench by my collar to make me a 'public example' my mom came to my rescue.

She glared at the scout lady and grabbed me by the hand. "We are leaving now." To me she said "We'll get lunch at the Dairy Queen out on the highway."

That was the end of my scouting experience.

Literal Box Cars

Even in the third grade we knew a lot about cars. Like the real life hot rod parked in our neighbor's driveway. It was a purple wreck with stenciled gold stars used in the weekend races on the old landing strip north of town. We knew the car was not street worthy because Red and his father-in-law loaded it on a flatbed to haul it to the races and it lacked a few important details like license plates, front fenders, and a muffler.

We had a couple of trikes, scooters, and an old pedal car cluttering up our yard, but nothing that even suggested speed and excitement. And speed and excitement seemed to be good cure for our summer doldrums. We did have the most important ingredient of all. Imagination.

Scrounging through the downtown alleys turned up a half dozen wooden crates. Nice big orange boxes and a tomato flat seemed the most promising, but we kept an open mind about the rest of the junk we drug home.

We lined the boxes up across the yard to help our visualization process. Details, we needed details. We begged a bunch of lids from my mom. Canning jar lids turned into headlights. Paint can lids substituted for wheels in a very adequate way since they didn't have to support anything or even turn. The steering wheel from the pedal car became the steering wheel for one of the box cars. Lard can lids from a neighbor's trash steered the other cars.

When my cousin and a neighbor girl joined our project, we decided to let each of us add personalized touches. I painted a smiling mouth and a button nose to the front of my box. Cousin Jimmy found an old chair cushion for a seat in his low slung tomato box. My brother added a backrest covered with an old rug.

We found a sack of old alphabet blocks to nail to the front panel of the boxes to serve as controls. Ha! We were off and racing.

For the rest of that week we made a terrific racket tearing around our imaginary race track, but sitting in an orange crate making car noises paled after awhile. We started bouncing the box cars around on the lawn. This escalated to crashes and soon we were mashing into each other to see who could demolish the other guy the quickest.

We made another expedition to find more boxes and transferred the accoutrements from the crashed cars to the new boxes. By the time my dad got home from work the front yard looked like the site of a small tornado. Splinters, broken boards, rags, papers everywhere and us kids duking it out in the middle of the mess.

We spent the next week recovering from our scrapes and bruises and cleaning up the mess. So much for excitement. We went back to playing hopscotch and marbles.

Horse of Glass, Horse of Ice

If you want your horses to last, then choose glass over ice. If you are looking for money value, then maybe ice would be your best choice. In 1942 my Auntie Carol and Grandma Hilma pooled their money to buy my mom a Christmas present, a pair of glass horse head bookends. It was a big deal for those two women to come up with the money or any money at all. My aunt was a nursing school student and Grandma was a housewife with an unemployed husband.

All my high school years the horses sat on the coffee table in the living room demanding to be dusted every day. By then they were nineteen years old. In 1961 I married and left home. The glass horses stayed behind to hold down the fort.

They celebrated their thirty fifth, fortieth, fiftieth, and sixtieth birthdays at my brother's house in Seattle. Then my brother decided the horses needed a new caretaker. He packed them up and brought them to my house on the Strait of Juan de Fuca.

I didn't have a coffee table for the glass horses but a handmade bench served admirably. They don't need dusting every day here, but I still greet them each morning and remember past years. Now as they are nearing their seventieth birthday, I wondered if they had become valuable after all this time.

I entered 'glass horse head bookends' into the search on E-bay. A dozen items came up on my computer screen. The price? About six bucks. Time does not always confer value on old stuff.

The ice horse was a whole different matter. We had a huge snow fall in Western South Dakota. Snow drifted and piled past the windows clear to the roof line. When the sun finally came out, we put on our snow suits and dug our way out of the house. While the other kids made snowmen, I decided to make a snow horse.

Three big snow balls the size of the bottom layer of a very large snowman made the body of the horse. We dribbled water over that base to make it solid. The horse's neck was an oblong snowball which we froze to the body with patience and more water. The head was harder. It kept falling off until we made thick reins to anchor it to the neck.

After the basic assembly was finished and fairly firm, I added eyes and nostrils of rock and carved a mane along its peculiar upright neck. The ears were over size, but added the finishing touch to the front end of the white beast. The tail was part of an old broom head and a towel acted as a saddle.

I tried to get the boys to make another one so we could race, but they had moved on to another project. I perched in the very cold saddle until my backside was about frozen. Along about that time the photographer from the Daily News happened by to catch pictures of what the storm had wrought. He came into the yard and snapped a few of me crouched on the snow horse.

Later the paper sent me a check for five dollars. My ice horse was worth almost as much as the glass bookend horses and lasted five days compared with the seventy years for the glass horses.

Stolen Horses

In 1960 I graduated from Pasco High School in Washington State. My Aunt Ardis had planned a trip back to South Dakota and she asked me to come along. Probably to keep her company on the long train ride. I packed up some undies, a nice dress [made by my aunt,] hair brush, tooth brush, and whatever socks I could find that didn't have wall-to-wall holes. Her husband, my Uncle John, drove us to Spokane where his sister, Jewel, lived. I spent the night sleeping on her couch and the next morning she drove us to the railroad station.

The train trip was uneventful. I had made the same trip a couple of years before with my family. At first I thought it was nice and peaceful traveling without my noisy brothers, but by the time we reached Missoula, Montana I was missing their chattering and games. My auntie hadn't sprung for a sleeper so we slept in our seats. We did eat in the dining car. That was new to me as we had always hauled a sack of eats along to save money. The most interesting thing about the dining car was the raised wooden edge of the table. It was supposed to keep your plate from sliding off the table when the train made a turn. It never seemed necessary.

About twenty hours out the forest view thinned out and then gave way to the flat expanse of the Great Plains. Eastern Montana and Northern South Dakota offered nothing to entertain the passengers. Eventually we arrived in Bowman, North Dakota the closest stop to Spearfish. A relative was waiting on the platform to drive us the hundred miles south to my grandmother's house.

The next few days were a blur of talking, drinking endless cups of coffee, mild arguments about our schedules and entertainment—a real snooze fest. Then my auntie decided I needed to visit my old chums in nearby Belle Fourche. Horrors. We finally found our old neighbor who had a daughter several years younger than me. She dumped me off to stay with them 'for a few days.' The big horse heist happened the next day.

Sherry and her friends were already bored with summer vacation and were hunting excitement. One of the boys borrowed his brother's car and we were off to the country. Racing over the hilly back roads was fun for an hour or so, then someone suggested we pay Mark Basdin a visit. He lived on a farm a few miles from town. We parked up the road out of sight and walked the last quarter of a mile with a lot giggling and back slapping.

The Basdin house sat smack in the middle of a big field. No yard, no landscaping, no driveway. A rusting tractor sat in knee high weeds nearby with an old car for company. We clomped across the rotting porch and banged on the door. No response so we walked right in. Empty except for a scrawny gray cat who fled through an open window. A spring broke couch and a TV set left on decorated the living room. Low ceilinged bedrooms led off from the high ceilinged main room. The kitchen with its piles of dirty dishes was a lean-to with a sloping roof. After a cursory look Sherry suggested a horseback ride. While the guys went out to check the horse population, Sherry hauled me into one of the bedrooms. A head high pile of clothing dominated the small space.

"Find a pair of jeans. You can't ride in that dress."

"Gross. Are they clean."

"Hurry up. I'll be outside."

I dug a possible pair of jeans from the pile and retreated to a corner where I hoped no one could see me. The house had no curtains or shades and all the windows were wide open.

By the time I got outside wearing the borrowed jeans under my dress, the boys had three horses bridled and were arguing about whether they should chance breaking into the tack room for saddles. They decided that might be a crime so it had to be a bareback ride.

There were six of us so we had to ride double. I ended up with the smallest boy and the tallest horse. At least that's what it felt like. We used an old oak stump for a mounting block and were soon clomping down the gravel road hooting and hollering. The horses were happy enough to be out in the sunshine. Or so it seemed.

About fifteen minutes down the road my boy decided he had to take his shirt off.

"Hot," he said.

"Wants me to feel him up," I thought.

He passed me the shirt which I secured under my thigh. My grip on his sweaty mid-section seemed less secure. The horse side-stepped and tossed his head. Maybe he agreed with me or, more likely, he was contemplating his hay net and oat bucket.

Sherry and her boy decided to gallop when we came to a level stretch of road. The rest of us followed. A witless bunch.

The shirt whipped out from under my leg and flapped my horse into a frenzy. Ten seconds later we were belly up in the ditch as the horse raced off into the woods. The other horses dumped their cargo and followed suit just as fast as their little brains could react.

We were a much deflated group trudging back to the car. I assume the horses made their way home, but I'll bet the family never did figure out why they were bridled and where the heck did Mark's favorite jeans disappear to.

Washington More or Less

The Basement

For years we lived next door to a den of iniquity and didn't know it. A high fence above a stone wall separated our small stucco house from our neighbors to the north. We heard the lady of the house shrieking at her two Pomeranian dogs a dozen times a day and a number of cars would be parked out front at all hours of the day and night. Still the husband held a steady job and served as a volunteer fireman all the years we lived there.

I returned to the neighborhood after a long absence to visit a childhood friend. After a few days of catching up on each other's lives she suggested we visit her friend Macy. I was uneasy about it because Macy lived with her grandmother in the house behind the tall fence. A place I had never been in all the years I had lived next door.

I half expected to be attacked by a hoard of yapping dogs when we approached the front door. Nothing. My friend laughed and said the dogs were long gone. Too many complaints and besides, the grandmother was too old to care for the little beasts.

Macy met us at the front door and led us through the house to the kitchen. "Granny's downstairs with the girls," she said and offered us sodas and chips. A racket from the direction of the basement stairs gave weight to her statement.

We chatted awhile before it was suggested we join the girls in the basement. I wondered how the old granny managed the narrow steps, but didn't mention it. Good thing too. Granny lolled in an oversize easy chair, a half ton of flab with newly permed and styled hair of an orange hue. Her dressing gown barely covered her ample front. She was giving instructions to three young women standing around a small table loaded with makeup, glittery bras and panties, ultra high heels, and hair pieces that looked like small furry animals.

"You , Tina. A little more spice. Try those gold heels and stretch pants."

Tina grabbed the heels and pants from the table and vanished behind a curtain across the end of the room.

"Ash and Juanita. Makeup. And more eye, more leg."

A child of about four ran around the room barefoot, still in her PJ's, blowing bubbles.

"Take the curlers out of Baby's hair" instructed Granny.

Macy grabbed the child and bent down to work on her hair, but Granny demanded "Stand her on the table."

We helped Macy clear the small table and hoist the child to center stage, then stepped back out of the way. Macy unwound the fat pink curlers to reveal bleached blond hair still kinky from a recent perm.

In the harsh light of a hundred watt bulb suspended from the ceiling the little girl looked like a Marilyn Monroe poser. The three girls emerged from their own makeovers and went to work on Baby.

One applied makeup including eye liner and mascara. It added to Baby's odd doll-like aura. Another girl stripped off Baby's PJ's and found a tiny version of an evening gown from a nearby box. She pulled it over the child's head, then twirled her around for Granny's inspection.

"She needs a bra," barked the old woman. "And panties"

I nudged my friend and asked what the heck was going on. She shushed me and went for another soda. While she was gone one of the girls produced a miniature pushup bra and removed the child's dress. Another girl applied a hefty smear of lipstick. Back on went the glittery dress. And voila! A miniature adult stood on the table.

"Shoes now," said Granny. "Not those slipper things. She's old enough to learn about heels."

Holding on to one girl's shoulder, the child wobbled a few steps.

"Put her down on the floor," said Granny. "No sense breaking the merchandise."

I bolted for the stairs with the bitter taste of incipient vomit in my mouth. The front door couldn't get there fast enough. I was still shaking when my friend joined me. "What is going on in there," I asked.

She shrugged and headed home.

Back of Hanford

We had spent many Sundays and holidays driving and hiking through the back roads of the Black Hills searching for the old mining town of Carbonate. We found the remains of many old towns and homesteads, but not our goal. Then, in August of 1955 we moved to Pasco, Washington. The place was mostly flatland desert. The only trees were the ones planted in living memory. The hills were merely sand dunes. No old gold mining towns here.

There was another old town that called to us though. The remains of old Richland, now part of the site of plutonium producing Hanford.

In the dim recess of history this area at the meeting place of the Yakima and Columbia Rivers was the site of the village of Wanapum. Several Indian tribes harvested salmon here. In October of 1805 Captain William Clark of the Lewis and Clark expedition paid a visit to Wanapum. He wrote "...there is no timber in sight except for small willow bushes in any direction..."

In 1904 a fellow named William Amon and his son Howard bought 2,300 acres of land on the north bank of the river for a town. From whom I don't know. Indians? The Feds? The State of Washington? He named it Richland. Not because he thought it was a rich land because it wasn't. Rather, he named it after a state legislator named Nelson Rich. Hmmm.

A couple hundred people made up the population of Richland all the years before 1943. A post office, general store, blacksmith shop, and a few clapboard houses made up the core of the town. Most residents supported themselves by fishing and dry land farming. A small scale irrigation system added some variety to the activity of this small community. Grapes in particular flourished with the added water.

Richland itself was bought by the US government in 1943 and the area turned into a bedroom community to house the workers at the country's first nuclear reactor. Though this site was heavily guarded and fenced, rumors of old structures on the other side of the river continued to circulate. The villages of White Bluffs and Hanford must have left some trace of their existence.

We began to drive the crumbling asphalt roads that ran north and south along the Columbia River across from the core of the plutonium producing operation. Most of these roads petered out after a few miles. Others ended at tall barred gates with warning signs. Still we persisted in our weekend exploration.

One weekend we went a bit too far down a sandy track and got mired in loose sand. That would have been a good time for one of the Hanford patrols to come by but none did. My dad finally freed the car by jacking it up, then pushing it off the jack until he had it turned around and the front end on more solid ground. Still we continued our exploration. Lewis and Clark had nothing on us for persistence.

One fall day we came to a gate across the road with all the usual barb wire and warning signs, but this one was different. A few feet into the tangle of sage brush and tumble weeds the fence was down.

We pulled the fence wire aside and drove very slowly around the gate and back onto the road which had thistles and prickly pear growing up through its cracks. Few if any vehicles had come this way for a very long time. We were now on the Hanford Reservation.

A mile or so farther along we came to a scattering of rickety rotting buildings. More radiation warning signs were nailed to the ancient structures. Otherwise things were probably just as they were when the citizens of White Bluff left in 1943. We searched through the mess that had been stores and houses, but found little. Two rusted metal advertising signs and some odd looking bottles which we stowed in the trunk of the car.

We were ready to leave when an open jeep with two armed soldiers came roaring out of the north. It wasn't the Indian attack that had plagued Lewis and Clark, but it was close enough. My dad apologized and we were escorted back to the gate. This time they unlocked it so we could drive right through. So much for exploring the dry land wilderness of south eastern Washington State. It was probably time for more profitable adult pursuits.

Dead in the Moses Lake Bus Station

I don't remember her name. The new girl in our art class at Pasco High School. I'll call her Beth. She showed up in mid September, a late transfer student. Her hair was carefully done and she dressed about like everyone else. She walked with a crutch because of a car accident in the spring. Probably the same accident that sent her to Pasco to live with her aunt and uncle.

We knew very little about her and Beth intended to keep it that way. She was a loner squared. Not a shy, keep to herself kind of loner, but rather the belligerent, don't touch me, don't talk to me, don't look at me kind of loner. It was hands off even for the kindly woman teaching the class.

We sat at tables to work on various projects. Beth sat across from me scribbling endless black slashes and whorls on her manila paper. Sometimes she got so wound up she made holes in her paper. Other times she wadded her paper into balls and threw them on the floor. We watched and said nothing.

One day we had a lesson on copper enameling. The teacher brought her own table top kiln and various supplies for us to use. She demonstrated painting the dull colored dust on a small bit of polished copper and firing it in the kiln to produce a vivid design. She displayed finished work made into ear rings, necklaces, tie clasps, and small mounted scenes.

When we lined up to select our copper cut outs and colors, Beth stormed to the head of the line and demanded to be first. The rest of us retreated and let her gather up the best stuff.

For the next couple of weeks Beth was almost human when she was working on her jewelry designs though no one was trusting enough to speak to her or even get close to her prickly, bristly demeanor. I'm sure the teacher breathed a prayer of relief.

None of our copper pieces came out as crisp and pretty as the teacher's, but most of us were satisfied. Not Beth. She hurled her finished work in the trash and clomped out of the room. We never saw her again. Except on TV.

As I was getting ready for school a few days after the incident in art class, my mom yelled at me to come see something. I joined her in the living room. "You know this girl?" She asked. I stood in front of the TV set and watched the news story. The banner streaming across the bottom of the screen read 'standoff with unidentified teenager.'

A newsman tried to explain the situation while a grainy black and white feed from a security camera played on the screen. It showed a room full of people scrambling back against the walls of a bus station. Some crouched under the pew-like benches. Others tried to open the windows or funnel out the narrow side door.

Another camera panned across the bus station waiting room with the sign 'Moses Lake' clearly in view. The commentator reported that they had been waiting for the 9:00 am bus to Spokane. Two police officers stood at one end of the room. Close by emergency personnel waited.

A girl with a crutch faced them. She wore a long overcoat and had a bag slung over one shoulder.

"It is Beth," I said to my mother. "What the heck is she doing in Moses Lake?"

"Nothing good," said my mom. "Those people are scared stiff."

"She wasn't in school yesterday."

Then, before we could say anything else, the girl in the overcoat raised her arm. She had a pistol, a big one. She swung around aiming it at the crowd and screaming something we could not hear.

The younger of the two police officers raised his own gun and shot Beth square in the forehead.

Art Class Again

You would think a high school art class a pretty tame place. Paper, paint, pencils. Draw this, paint that. Gee, that's pretty. Gad, what a mess. A little poking, a few punches, some goofing off. How hard could it be. It was the lazy student's paradise.

That spring term the class was a mixture of juniors and seniors, thirty-two in number. The girls sat at the tables closest to the teacher's desk, the guys mostly sat in back. Except for Jack. He sat with the girls. We figured girls were the only reason he signed up for art class. One particular girl. Elsie Jameson was the focus of his attention.

Jack had dated Elsie the year before, but she broke it off right after Christmas. Trouble was Jack refused to accept the break up and followed Elsie everywhere. Called her morning, noon, and night. Sent her candy, sent her flowers, sat on her doorstep hours on end until her father called the police.

Still, Jack persisted. Most of us girls were familiar with the teenage boy who didn't recognize the word 'no,' but we also knew that this thing with Jack was a couple of levels below normal.

Elsie remained aloof. She refused to talk to Jack and after a month or so of his bad behavior, she refused to talk to anyone. I think she got tired of apologizing for the way he elbowed his way past us to claim the chair next to her, for the way he hissed at us to get lost and give him some room with his 'honey,' for his total disregard for the teacher's attempts at keeping him at bay.

Finally the principal intervened and Jack was kicked out of the class. After sitting in the hallway all week waiting to torment Elsie after class, he was expelled from school. Hall monitors were told to report his presence should he darken the door of the school again. He still managed to get in now and then, but the assistant principal, an ex-marine, made short work of sending him packing.

Elsie's mother would wait by the school door to take her home and we felt sure the problem was solved. Elsie seemed to relax a bit and joined in some of the class discussions about famous painters. We finished the school year on an even keel. I graduated and enrolled at the junior college. Elsie started her senior year and we lost touch.

In October the newspaper's lead story was headlined 'Pasco High School Girl Missing.' Elsie's car was found abandoned on the new Columbia River bridge. Doors open, papers, and purse contents strewn around, but no sign of anyone. A day later her body was found on a sand bar a short distance downstream.

Jack was arrested immediately. His flash flattened stare dominated the morning paper. A bloody hammer turned up in the trash at his apartment.

The autopsy results escalated Elsie's death many notches up the scale of brutality. Elsie was damaged, but still alive when she was thrown off the bridge to drown.

Whiskey on the Water
Or Man, Is That a Big Fish

A few days before Fourth of July weekend my Uncle Hubert called from Seattle. He said they had rented a cabin on Whidbey Island. Would we like to make the drive from Pasco to Seattle and join them for a sort of reunion.

So when my dad got off work on Thursday we piled into the car and headed over the mountains. My mom had baked an angel food cake which we stowed in a cardboard box in the trunk along with a suitcase with our change of clothes, toothbrushes, etc. We dropped the canary in his cage at my aunt's house on our way out of town.

It was almost dark by the time we pulled into Hubert's driveway. The uncles were trying to hitch a boat and trailer to my cousin Leonard's car while other cousins stashed a mass of fishing tackle in the trunk. The women were packing up food, utensils, clothing and bedding . Everyone seemed to have a different idea of what was a priority. Three electric frying pans seemed to be high on the list.

Nearly everyone thought it was important to take as few vehicles as possible. My brother and I ended up in the backseat of a car between two large aunts with the cake on my lap. It was decided that we would follow Leonard driving the boat pulling car. It would be easier to keep track of the boat in the traffic.

Boy were they right about the traffic. It was wall-to-wall from south Seattle to the turn off to the ferry. Everybody was heading somewhere. Fast. We ran about three red lights and took a short cut the wrong way down a one way street. We would have ended up in the pokey if the cops hadn't been so busy elsewhere.

We were the last car on the ferry. The guy behind us offered a hundred bucks if we would let him go ahead, then got threatening and belligerent at our refusal.

It was dark by the time we bumped up the road to the rented cabin. Three cars and a boat and one small parking space. We got unsquashed and hauled our junk into the small cabin. One of the aunts took over and ordered the fishing gear, clam shovels, and boots back to the car and the boat to the dock. We still took up more than our share of the space, but tried to ignore it.

The cabin was a bare bones affair with no interior walls and wiring snaking across the ceiling to power a few bare bulbs in each of the two bedrooms and the main room. The kitchen was a sink, beat up old frige, a two burner propane stove, and a bit of counter space. No wonder we brought the electric frying pans along.

They bundled us kids together in a couple of sleeping bags in the corner of one of the bedrooms, then spent the night playing cards and drinking beer. And keeping us awake. We were a miserable bunch at our breakfast of cornflakes and milk next day. Warm milk because beer took precedence and the milk had sat out on the counter all night. Hangovers and lack of sleep made the grownups a testy bunch.

But it was a holiday and we got on with holiday stuff. The aunts went off to dig clams on the beach. Big ugly things, not the slick greeny brown razor clams we dug at Long Beach and Grayland. My brother and I trailed along behind them hunting shells and junk washed by the tide, but soon discovered there was nothing of interest to be found.

Next we paid a visit to the docks where we could hear loud music coming from several of the yachts, but little activity. We headed inland. The road scooting from the cove led to a small convenience store and beyond that a chain link fence with a locked gate. We already knew that the road to the ferry dock held nothing of interest so we returned to the cabin.

Cousin Leonard was dumping the morning's clam harvest into a box of cornmeal to clean themselves out. Hubert had just climbed out of bed and was intent on adding some fish to our diet. He wanted Leonard to go with him, but had to settle for me and my brother. Leonard did walk down to the dock to help launch the boat.

The boat had seemed big while it was bouncing along behind Leonard's car on the highway. Maybe it had shrunk when it hit the water. We sat in the bow seat and Uncle sat in back where he manned the engine and the steering thing. He passed us a couple of extra heavy fishing poles, opened his whisky flask, and steered out of the cove.

Once on the open water he cut the engine to a slow idle and we threw our lines out. The sun came out and gleamed the water. It also gave us a pretty fair sunburn. Oblivious to sun or shiny water Uncle swigged his flask and steered even farther from the cove. Conversation was nonexistent especially after I asked Uncle if the boat had life jackets. And if he knew how to swim. He answered by hacking and spitting over the side, then taking another swig of whiskey.

My meditation on the depth of the water stopped when my brother's pole took a vicious dip. Fish, he screamed. Uncle climbed over me to help hold the pole whose nose was now under water. The boat slewed sideways, then took off after the fish. It was a real battle. Just like in the movies. Finally the humongous brown creature landed in the bow of the boat. Uncle thunked it on the head and it lay still.

With Uncle's instruction I turned the boat shoreward and we trolled back to the cove. It seemed like a very long, slow trip, but our reception back at the cabin erased the unease and discomfort of our day on the water.

The fish was examined and measured, then Uncle and Leonard strung it up from a tree out front. Other campers came by and exclaimed over it. Then it was cleaned, wacked up, and added to the other supper finds.

By late afternoon the electric frying pans were heating with gobs of Crisco in each one. Breading for the fish and clams waited on wax paper along the counter. The beer flowed freely.

We filled our plates and went outside to eat. Somewhere between the last bite of fish and the first bite of chocolate angel food an Auntie ran out of the cabin screaming Fire, Fire. We all raced into the cabin to see the electric wires in the ceiling sprouting flames. Too much cooking, too many electric frying pans. Yikes. One of the more sober men threw the breaker and pulled the offending wires out into the yard. Disaster averted.

They aired out the cabin and ran an extension cord to the next door cabin to make coffee. No card playing and beer drinking for the night. I spent the evening on the pier listening to the hullabaloo from the from the various cabin cruisers tied up there and watching the moon come up. We packed up and went home the next morning.

More Horsing Around or a Sacajawea Picnic

Sacajawea Park is a small splotch of green southeast of Pasco, Washington in the crotch of the 'Y' where the Snake River joins the Columbia. The Lewis and Clark expedition camped on the site October 16th to 18th, 1805. This small oasis was deeded to the park system in 1931.

We often packed a picnic lunch and drove to the park on the outskirts of Pasco to eat. It was a nice irrigated bit of green in the otherwise barren desert of the surrounding countryside. Not the beauty of South Dakota's Black Hills that we had been used to, but still, an oasis amongst the sand dunes and tumbleweeds of Eastern Washington.

A number of other families had spread out blankets and coolers around us, but we paid them no mind. Today we had fried chicken and potato salad which we scarfed down like we hadn't eaten in days. About the time we were about to tuck into carrot cake with cream cheese icing my wannabe boy friend showed up.

"What you want, Gene?"

"Come have a nice horseback ride with me," he said. "You know you're crazy about horses."

"I don't think they allow horses in the park."

"Come on. We can ride to my grandma's place and your folks can pick you up there."

"And where might that be," said my dad.

"Right on the highway into town. We'll take a short cut cross country."

I finally decided to go with Gene, so after more interrogation from my dad as to the location of Grandmother's house we set out for the horse.

"She should be just over this dune," said Gene. But no horse. "Guess I got mixed up."

We slogged over a couple more dunes before we found the chestnut mare with her saddle slightly askew and dragging her bridle reins.

"Did you actually tie her up with the reins." I held up the broken end of one of them.

"Hold her while I straighten this out." Gene gave the saddle a tug, then put his whole weight into it.

"You need to re-saddle her. Man, it's hot out here."

"I'll get it. Just gimme a minute." The horse side-stepped in a tight circle around us with Gene yanking at the saddle with all his might.

"You're irritating her."

"She's used to me."

"Like a big blow fly."

With the saddle somewhat in place Gene heaved himself to the mare's back. She grunted and snorted a bit then settled down. Sweat rivualed down her neck and mine.

"Gimme the reins and climb on," said Gene. He was fumbling for the stirrups and missed the daggers I was looking at him.

"You got to be kidding."

"There's a big rock over there. You can stand on that."

"Well, get over there."

The rock seemed a bit precarious, but I stepped onto it and waited for my rusty knight to maneuver the horse into position.

"Wrong side you dumb ass. Can't mount a horse from the right."

"Sorry." Sweat dripped off Gene's nose and his shirt was soaked by now. "She don't turn so good."

"Now get your foot out of that stirrup. I need it. And hold her steady."

When the mare felt the added weight behind the saddle, she started circling in tight formation her head down and ears back.

"You sure she's used to carrying double?"

"Of course. How hard can it be."

"Get her head up you dufus."

No use. The horse dumped us both in the sandy gulley and took off for home showering us with clods as a parting insult.

"Now what?" I said.

"Guess we walk."

"Honest to Pete." We struggled out of the gulley. The horse was long gone. Gene took off through the tumbleweeds while I dusted myself off. "Hey, come back here. That's the wrong way."

He stopped and came back. "How do you know?"

"Listen. You can hear the trucks over on the highway."

By the time we reached the highway we were sweat city. My hair dripped and I could tell I was brewing a good sun burn. We finally crossed the black top strip and walked up Grandma's driveway. My dad wavered between relief and anger. Gene's grandma opted for outright screaming furry. Mostly for the treatment of the horse and the missing saddle. Ditched by the horse enroute.

I climbed in the back seat where my brother scrunched in the corner reading a comic book. The air conditioning nearly froze me. Froze my feelings for guys in general and one in particular for sure.

V. Down On The Farm-Southern Illinois

Two Yellow Kitties

Over the years I had two yellow tom cats. As is often the case with short haired yellow cats, the two looked like twins. They were born 25 years and more than a thousand miles apart, but twins for sure.

In the spring of 1947 my mom and I were staying in Spearfish, South Dakota with my grandmother while my dad finished his GI Bill course in Missouri. When new people moved into the empty house across the highway from us, they brought their very pregnant mama cat with them. The cat elected to have her kittens in our shed. Four tiny damp babies. One grey, one black, one a speckled calico, and one yellow one.

We fawned over the babies and tried to befriend the mamma cat, but she shunned our attention and returned to her real family each day to be fed. One day when the kittens were old enough to stretch their legs, yawn, and make tentative steps around their nest under the work bench, their mama was hit and killed by a car while crossing the highway.

We went to house across the highway to inquire about the future of the kittens, but they wanted nothing to do with them. The babies were now our responsibility. We fed them with an eye dropper for a week or so, then persuaded them to eat canned cat food. In nothing flat they were tearing around the yard and into everything.

My mom said I could choose one to keep. We found homes for the other three. Well I remember the day we delivered the first of the kittens to its new home. I sat in the back seat of our old

Chevy with the kitten, wrapped in a frayed towel, on my lap while my mom drove the seven miles to Belle Fourche.

Up a steep hill, down a gravel drive and there was the kitten's new home. A girl about my own age was waiting and took the kitten from me. I was sad for a few miles, then remembered the three kittens waiting for me at home.

The other people that were promised kittens stopped by the house to pick them up later that week. My yellow kitten seemed lonesome and stopped eating for a few days, but a dinner of extra stinky cat food perked him right up.

Soon after Yellow Kitty started eating again, my dad came home from Missouri, his courses complete. He had a job waiting for him in Belle Fourche so we started looking for a house. Me and Yellow Kitty stayed with my grandma while they cleaned and moved our stuff into the new old house.

We liked our new house even though it was old and clunky. It was all ours and we didn't have to share it with anyone else. After my dad had come home from the Navy we had stayed with a series of relates, uncles, aunts, cousins, grandparents because there was no available housing in all of western South Dakota. Even Yellow Kitty seemed content.

Me and my little brother got our money's worth from that cat. We dressed him up in old baby clothes and trundled him around the house and yard in a rickety old carriage. We teased him and loved him and lugged him around the neighborhood. He was a mainstay in our games of house and war alike. That cat could serve as a baby one minute, a prisoner of war the next.

But kittens and kids grow up. Some sooner than others. Yellow kitty took to scouting the neighborhood by himself. He seemed quite content to spend his days lounging on the couch, sleeping and eating and purring, but at nightfall he demanded to be let out.

He courted the lady cats with fervor and often came home with torn ears and missing clumps of hair. Sometimes the battles with other toms happened under our very windows and my dad would go out and douse the combatants with a bucket of cold water. At certain times of the year he would stay away for days at a time and the neighborhood rumor had him moved in with another family up the hill. One without children to torment him and a lady cat for him to play with.

As we made plans to move to Washington, we saw less and less of Yellow Kitty. He seemed to sense that change was in the air. He was getting up in years, nearly seven by now. We planned to take him with us, but he had other ideas. After an absence of a month or more we paid a visit to the elderly couple up the hill on the off chance of finding Yellow Kitty. And sure enough—there he was ensconced on a plump pillow washing his face after a lunch of sardines.

The couple insisted they would provide our cat a good and loving home. No arguments from us. Yellow Kitty would have hated a four day ride in a cramped car and I doubt if he would have liked that dry and dust swept part of the world. Hopefully he lived happily ever after.

My next yellow tom cat was nearly thirty years later. My husband and I had moved to a farm on the Big Muddy River in Southern Illinois. Before the movers finished unloading our stuff we started collecting animals. A scruffy white dog was the first, then friends moving back east asked us to take their cat. She proved to be pregnant and soon delivered four snuffling, mewling kittens.

One baby was a black and gray tiger stripe, one was white with gold and black spots, number three was black, and biggest of all was a yellow one. Yellow Kitty reincarnated.

With no children to monopolize his time with silly games, this Yellow Kitty grew up to be a mighty hunter and avid lover before the end of his first year.

He started small with barn mice and grasshoppers. Before Christmas he brought his first rat to lay at my front door. Had he been a human and a church goer, he would have been ostracized for the sin of pride. Fortunately cats rarely draw the ire or even the attention of busy body congregations concerned with the sins of their neighbors.

One of the high points of Yellow Kitty's hunting career was his battle with a huge snake. The snake appeared in the front yard one morning after the river had reached flood stage. Coiled and spitting the snake defied my attempts to grab it for a speedy return to the muddy water.

Yellow Kitty jumped in with all four feet. After much thrashing about the cat got the snake in a choke hold, shook it a few times, then deposited the writhing creature at my feet as if to say 'there's how it's done.' I grabbed it behind the head and carried it across the pasture to the river. Unhurt, the snake slithered away downstream.

Yellow Kitty Two had a distinct advantage over Kitty One. All of his lady friends lived on the premises. None of the neighbors had cats to tempt him away from home and he actually had his paws full taking care of the resident lady cats. It took a lot of cat power to keep Nile Creek free of marauding varmints and he kept the supply of new kittens up to snuff for many years.

Cows to be Milked

The day dragged on and on with the two lawyers arguing minute points of rules and regulations. Three jurors were yet to be selected. The judge excused a handful of potentials with critical jobs and an ailing child. The rest of us squirmed on the hard benches thinking bad thoughts about the judge, the justice system, the accused, and the lawyers.

Outside, the beautiful spring day waited to expire with the last rays of sun spreading red across the landscape. The lights came on in the courtroom. Some lackey passed out half cups of hours old coffee and glazed donuts. The lawyers continued to badger the next in line without visible progress.

When darkness obliterated the red sun streaks outside the window, I could stand no more. My butt ached and my brain felt like yesterday's oatmeal. At the next break I approached the judge and waited to be recognized. When he looked my way, I blurted out, "There's cows to be milked."

"Excused," he answered.

I fled the court room leaving my sweater and book behind. A small price to pay for freedom. Later my husband asked how I could lie so glibly to a judge. I told him it wasn't a lie. Jackson County was full of cows waiting to be milked.

Calf in the Backseat, Piggies in the Trunk

When we moved to the country we were driving a 1965 Ford. Though we soon added an old pickup truck to our inventory, it didn't help with all the hauling the farm required. Small critters like baby calves and piglets could not be trusted to ride safely in the back of that truck. Just the thought of one of those animals splatted on the road was frightening.

A neighbor a few miles from us mentioned that he had a three day old calf from one of his milkers for sale. He bred his first calf Holstein heifers to a small angus bull to make that first calf smaller and less trouble for cow and owner alike. If we were interested, the calf would cost us twenty five bucks and we had to pick it up that evening.

We removed the back seat of the Ford and my husband took off up the hill to get the calf. Three day old calves are considerably larger than you would imagine, especially when they were thrashing all four legs and butting everything in sight with their very hard heads.

When he pulled into the driveway, the calf had her head over the front seat drooling ropes of spit over everything. We finally extracted the squirming beast from the car and my husband carried her to the barn. I got the bottle of formula I had mixed up earlier and followed them. It took a few tries, but we finally got the calf in a good grip and she got the hang of the nipple in nothing flat. A month later she was boss of the farm.

The baby pigs were harder to deal with. Pigs, it seems, have a lot less places for a good grip and give the general feeling of being slippery. When a local breeder called to tell us he had several cull piglets for us, the old Ford still smelled like cow. When we got to the pig farm, the owner led us to a small concrete floored pen away from the main buildings.

We leaned over a newly whitewashed fence to look at the cull pigs. They were considerably bigger than we expected. Big enough to barbeque if that was your thing. The thought of sixty pounds of squeal trying to climb into the driver's seat was too much. We put the duo in the trunk for the eight mile trip home. Every bump and corner was punctuated by thumps and squalls, but we all made the trip safely.

We drove as close to the new pigpen as we could to transfer the pigs to their new home. Not close enough to suit either pigs or pig handler, but it was a real hoot watching my husband wrap his arms around the middle of a pig and lug it through the gate. The second pig was bigger and bouncier, but its flapping ears made a good hand hold and it was soon installed in the fine new pen.

The pigs were immediately happy with their new quarters because they had dirt. And mud. And the remains of last year's garden to root around in. They cared not one wit that the black heifer had declared king of the hill.

The Daffodil Path

Our land followed the Big Muddy River for nearly a mile. It was a narrow strip of river bottom flanked by hills covered with a tangle of trees, kudzu, and poison ivy, a 200 acre piece of Southern Illinois or Little Egypt as it was called. Most of the land in that forgotten part of the state had been deeded to homecoming Civil War soldiers on their return from fighting. It proved to be an empty gesture on the part of the government.

The small plots of land were not capable of supporting the most hardworking farmer. Let alone a family. After a few years of hard work and worry, most found work in town or turned to some home based trade like harness making, horse shoeing, or even the distilling bootleg whiskey.

By the time we bought the land the small holdings had been consolidated into one bigger parcel. The land that routinely flooded twice a year and supported fast growing crops of head high horse weed, smothering kudzu, and every biting insect known to man still could not support two people and a small bunch of domestic animals.

The rough overgrown hills hid many secrets and served them up reluctantly and seldom. I stumbled onto one such hidden place on an early spring day. The old home site would have been invisible except for the few days each year that the daffodils bloomed.

The nodding yellow flowers formed a path through the underbrush. And when I knew where to look a tangled red flowered bush and a gnarly old apple tree appeared. Blocked by long downed trees and a mats of poison ivy vine, I tried to go around, but was thwarted by a hidden mess of wire and rotted posts. I decided to go home for tools and some help. Deep cellars and cisterns dotted these hills with treachery. This was no place to be exploring alone.

Before I turned away from the path of daffodils I stopped to listen to the hilltop conversation.

First the birds and the gentle wind spoke of long ago days when children's voices and women singing caressed the air, then the daffodils spoke. First to the red bush flowers they sang, no one comes here anymore. The red bush answered, it's been a long, long time. The old apple tree leaned in to remark that its fruit had fed only the deer and the rabbit for fifty years or more.

This homestead that had once given shelter to a family now lays a crumpled, rotting mess. The red bush warned that the pathway marked by the daffodils leads through an invisible door to an empty cellar, deep and dark.

Maybe someone will come to build walls and floor, a roof to hold out the storm, said the daffodils to the red bush. Why asked the red bush. The road is long covered with fallen trees. Rocks and washouts cover the last ruts of the road to town.

I closed my eyes to better see the picture of long ago life on the hill top with its foggy view of the Mississippi River, but nothing appeared. I kicked the mound of debris near the daffodil lane. Moldy traces of a life left behind emerged. A broken China plate, a worn leather shoe, a hoe without a handle, and deep in the pile a toy truck of tin with no wheels. The things left behind. One could only hope that a new life opened up for these folks when they journeyed off the mountain.

Or perhaps they found work on the assembly line at a nearby shoe factory. Or hired out to pick fruit at the many orchards in the valley. The daffodils cried that they should have stayed in the freedom and fresh air of the hilltop, but the apple tree knew better.

I unearthed a few of the daffodil bulbs and carried them home to plant beside my own path. Where are they now?

The Postman Brings Stuff

In the 1970's and 80's we lived off the beaten track in the hills of southern Illinois. No TV, gravel roads, a produce your own food mentality, and a growing fear of impending doom pervaded the area. We had two hundred acres to raise food, livestock, and feed for those animals. Still, we did need connections with the real world. One of these was the mail.

Back in the good old days, before the US Postal Service initiated the little mail delivery vehicles we see today, country mailmen used their own vehicles to bring the mail. Ours was no exception. Our mailman, Greg, had an old broke down Chevy. The fenders were rusty and dented, the windshield a spider web of cracks. The front seat springs left the driver nearly sitting on the floor and peering through the spokes of the steering wheel.

Greg lived in a nearby commune where all things were shared. Still, somebody had to work and he was one of the appointed workers. All of the postal service mottos applied because he was on his route through all sorts of weather and all manner of road conditions. He and his fellows kept that old car tuned and purring no matter how bad it looked.

Greg, and probably everyone else in the commune read my magazines before they appeared in my mailbox. Sometimes my Western Horseman came with bits of popcorn between the pages and the Mother Earth News arrived in shreds. A friend asked why I didn't complain. Good reason, I answered.

Like the day our first order of honey bees came. I could see the mob of dark bees in Greg's car as he slowly drove down the hill and into our driveway. The container of bees had jarred open at one corner somewhere after it left the farm supply place in Missouri. Without complaint our valiant mailman removed the bees from his backseat and placed them very carefully in our carport along with the usual junk mail and bills.

The next incident involved baby chicks. One hundred and ten cheeping, pooping little creatures. Fifty straight run Barred Rocks, fifty Buff Orpington hens, and ten speckled Araucana. They arrived safe and sound at my front door in early spring.

And then there was the dust. After Mount St. Helens blew her stack out in Washington State, the residents experienced a surfeit of volcanic ash. My mom filled an envelope with the stuff she brushed off her car after the blast and mailed it to me. By the time Greg got that one to my mailbox both he and his car had a fine layer of ash on every surface. I expect he spent the rest of his route coughing and spitting. My next magazine had stab marks on it.

Dust

May of 1980. Sweltering hot and clear blue skies in Little Egypt. That's what this part of Southern Illinois is called. We had named our hilly farm Nile Creek. It is a mess of small fields, poison ivy infested woods, and our collection of livestock.

It is Saturday morning and the cats are waiting to be fed. They follow me to the mailbox.

When I open the box, a cloud of gray dust pours out. Good grief pussy cats. What the heck is this? On top of the usual catalogues and fliers is an envelope with a Washington State postmark. It seems to be the source of the dust. With the cats following I take the mail up to the house. I place it on the kitchen table and give it the eye as I mix up the cats' kibble and canned fishy food.

The white envelope was still puffing a bit of dust when I returned from the barn where the cats were scarfing down their morning meal. From the handwriting I knew the envelope was from my mother in Pasco, a dreary town in Eastern Washington.

I put the envelope in a plastic mixing bowl and opened it carefully. No note, no explanation. Just a good sized pile of fine grained, gritty dust. I put a lid on the bowl and left it sitting on the end of the table sure that an explanation would follow.

A few days later the letter of explanation arrived. I imagine the mailman had handled the envelope with the Washington postmark with care and trepidation. My mom reported that the dust was from the volcanic eruption of Mount St. Helens. What volcano eruption I wondered. Far from TV or even a news reporting radio station, I must have missed that story.

She wrote that over on the west side of the state on May 18th the bright spring sky had turned dark as night when a column of ash from the distressed mountain shot 80,000 feet in the atmosphere. By noon the whole state was dark as night as tons and tons of ash settled on everything. Airports, roads, and businesses came to a grinding halt.

She had scooped the ash off the hood of her car in the days after that terrible event. And mailed it to me. I put the stuff in a test tube with a cork stopper and added it to my collection of memorabilia.

In the meantime I owed the mailman an apology. We didn't have those spiffy mail vehicles in those days so he's probably still cleaning dust out of his car. And his jeans and his shoes and his nose.

Red Horse Leaving

After years of collecting horse statuettes, pictures, and books, going to races and rodeos alike, I bought a real live horse. Was it fun? I don't really know. Is a rough, teeth clacking ride through a mountainous countryside fun? Or a screaming descent on an old carnival rollercoaster? Life with the red horse had been that and so much more.

The red horse was my first horse. He seemed to be a poor candidate for a first horse or even a second or third horse. A pushy acquaintance of mine had coaxed, connived and railed at me until I finally bought the tall chestnut horse. Too tall, but that had been the least of his faults.

The first time I saw the beast he was standing knee deep in the mud of a much patched old corral. His ribs stood out and his mane and tail were a twisted mass of cockleburs and filth. He barely noticed when we poked at him and pried open his mouth to check his teeth. 'He's just down from the track,' said his owner. 'Thoroughbred of course.'

'Sure. And I'm queen of England,' I muttered. The red horse cocked a hind foot as if to kick. Probably his comment on world affairs. 'How much?'

'Two hundred bucks and I'll haul him for you."

We agreed on one-seventy-five, hauling, and a new set of shoes.

The red horse settled in quickly. We clipped his mane and hosed him down. Mostly we fed him. In return he became wild and overbearing. He kicked and chewed on his pasture mates at the boarding stable until the other owners complained. He stood quietly to be brushed and saddled, but became a wild-eyed nut case with a rider up. To slow down his urges to run away with a rider up we pulled his shoes and rode him barefoot. Time and training had little effect. Sore feet helped more.

We moved the red horse to the farm where he had plenty of room to run and only a few companions to pick on. The clincher was New Years day when I was moving him to a different pasture. With a sudden whirl he jerked the lead rope from my hand, gave a snort, and kicked me square in ribs. The red beast just didn't like me. I let the word out that he was for sale.

A student at the university, a girl from Chicago, thought she could make a jumper out of him and paid my asking price contingent on the results of the vet check.

The red horse acted the perfect gentleman when the vet ran his hands over him, looked at his teeth, lifted each hoof, and listened to his heart and lungs with a stethoscope. 'No problems,' he said. 'All problem,' I whispered to myself. 'How do you find a problem with a problem.'

Chicago girl didn't want to take delivery until Easter break. The red horse was turned out in a back pasture to wait. Spring rains raised the river level to record heights and the red horse seemed stranded by the water across the road to the back of the farm. Very deep water and heavy overflow from the nearby sewage plant made crossing the creek impossible. The red horse would have to go overland.

So up the steep hillside with its thick coat of poison ivy, berry briars, and kudzu we climbed. Thrashing and snorting the horse mostly dragged me the last little way up the hill. We had an easy stretch across the ridge of the hill to catch our breath, then it was downhill in a long slippery diagonal. The next obstacle, a barb wire fence, came next.

No going around, under, or over with a horse in tow so I pulled the staples from the wire on a few of the posts and forced the fence to the ground. Rocks to hold the wire down and a scrap of lumber from a nearby dump site to cover it and I had a highway for the horse.

123

The fence crossed, I tied the horse to a branch and put the fence back up as much as possible. It would take some work later. The next stretch looked easy. I scratched the red horse behind the ears and he bumped me gently with his big head. Maybe he liked me a little after all.

With the road in sight we slowed to an amble. The horse's hooves kicked up last fall's dry leaves as we moved across the face of the wooded hill. We paused to look at the sun on the river below and the path we had made. A few early daffodils lay askew along the way. Maybe this was all a big mistake. Leaving wasn't all it was cracked up to be.

125

Camping, Camping

When spring quarter at Southern Illinois University moved from lectures to final exams, we got the bright idea of camping our way back to the Washington coast. Think of all the money we'd save bypassing the motels along the way.

My husband asked me if I'd ever gone camping. Once with some elderly neighbors I remembered. We drove up into the National Forest where they put up their big tent and a tiny pup tent for me. We sat around eating sandwiches from their cooler and drinking. Orange pop for me and whiskey neat for them.

Around midnight they asked me if there was anything else I needed, then crawled off to bed without hearing my answer. I wanted to shout a good hotel with room service. Or at least a drive in restaurant and a room with walls and a bed. I spent the night on that bumpy ground listening to loud snoring and waiting for the bears to carry me off to supper. Their supper.

But I refrained from informing my beloved about my disenchantment with camping. Instead I told him I couldn't think of any place to buy gear. Unfortunately the Montgomery Ward catalog store said they could supply us with anything we needed.

We started work on the LIST. Tent—no little pup tent though. Something you could stand up in and floor and a door. Sleeping bags. Shouldn't need expensive ones. After all it was summer. Something to cook on, a cooler, a lantern, a cook set, folding chairs. A whole load of stuff to fit into the car trunk. Turned out it didn't fit and so we went back to Wards and ordered a car top carrier.

Our stuff from Ward's arrived a few days before we were to leave. By the time we got it all unpacked we had a mountain of plastic bags and wrapping material. We would have been better off taking the trash on our trip and leaving the camping stuff at the curb for the garbage man.

But we persisted. The day before we were to leave we decided to practice putting up the tent. Who ever thought a tent could have so many parts. We laid it out flat and tackled staking it down. The bendy little stakes went every which way on their way into the hard ground. We added a hammer to our camping kit. The exterior aluminum poles proved to be a puzzle only a third grader could solve. Six beers later the tent slouched crookedly while we sat in our new lawn chairs toasting our success.

The lantern was another matter. I refused to get close to the thing. My husband had another beer and then gave the lantern a big drink of fuel. Next he tackled the instruction sheet. Step one was to install some little gauzy things he called 'mantles.' And what did the instructions say about this important step. 'Tie the mantles on right.' Gee, thanks.

That was enough practicing for us. If we couldn't get the lantern and the stove working, we could stop for takeout and sit in the dark to eat it. We added a small grill and a bag of briquettes to our pile.

Take off day came way too soon. We had a late start and made it as far as a small park west of St. Louis about a hundred miles from home. We decided to put off messing with the more cantankerous gizmos and opted for steaks from the market. We got them grilling while we put up the tent and turned to check on them in time to see a large dog plow into the grill and make off with half our supper in his mouth. Real roughing it, I'd say.

Next day we drove for miles across the rest of Missouri and the plains of Kansas. We set up camp in the city park of a tiny town near the Colorado border. We were well ogled by the entire population before we closed the tent flap and slept through a good sized thunder storm. At least we found that the tent actually was water proof.

Next stop was a campground in Wyoming. The wind blew so hard we tied the tent to the carrier on the car. We did get a shower at this stop though, so all was not lost.

Montana was cold, very, very cold. I bought a warmer sleeping bag, but it didn't help much. By the time we reached Three Forks water in the tent was freezing at night. Me too. We bought a tent heater that cost the price of a night at a good motel. It warmed things up but put out enough nasty fumes to earn it classification as a secret weapon.

The next night we landed at a wilderness camp ground with huge trees and a rushing stream. Very beautiful. We battened down the hatches and went to bed. Not too hot, not too cold, good supper, fewer bumps and ridges under the sleeping bag, porta potty nearby and reasonably clean. Maybe camping wasn't so bad after all.

About one o'clock clanking noises woke me up. I crawled out of my warmish bed and unzipped the tent door. A brown bear stared back at me. Startled he climbed a few feet up a handy tree and clung there with his long claws. The moonlight made his eyes shine yellow.

Not wanting to turn my back on the intruder, I roused my husband with a loud whisper. He assured me that the bear was more frightened than I was. No way. Old golden eyes wasn't the least bit frightened. I grabbed my bedding and edged around the tent very, very slowly. I kept eye contact with the intruder until I felt the door handle, then I took a deep breath and dived into the car. I spent the rest of the night with my sleeping bag over my head. I listened to the creature clanking the trash cans together until I finally fell asleep.

The next morning the park rangers came with a barrel trap on the back of a pickup truck. They caught old yellow eyes and hauled him away. I stood in the road to bid him adieu. I also said goodbye to camping.

V. On The Road

When Is A Palace Not A Palace

Florence, Italy in the fall. Our host met us at the train to take us to our apartment. His first words were innocent enough, but still stirred a feeling of unease in me.

"We thought you'd get the flavor of Florence in an old property, a palace, rather than one of the newer flats."

"How old?"

" The family that owns it live there, but rent out two street level apartments"

"In a palace?"

"The palace was built in 1870 for an Englishman named Fredrick Wilson. He was an artist."

We squeezed into one of the smallest cars ever. Luckily we had almost no baggage. A small backpack and a day bag. On the high speed, tire screeching trip from the station to the apartment we learned that the synagogue next door to the palace wasn't built until 1882. Florence was the capital city of Italy at that time, then when the government moved to Rome, the palace was sold to the Gattai family, ancestors of the present owners.

After a knuckle biting run the wrong way of a one way street 'to save time,' we arrived at a two story building on a quiet street. Gray stone decorated the first floor and framed the door to the street and the second story windows. A tall iron grill guarded the street door from intruders. Less decorative grills covered the ground floor windows.

 With a lot of key clanking our host got us into the building. The dark foyer was a jumble of old and new. A huge spiral staircase worthy of a queen wound up one side of the space some twenty feet into a halo of light. A half dozen bicycles leaned against the base of a marble column. A jumble of umbrellas and rain boots spilled out of a corner. We stood near the door to the first apartment waiting for our host to find the next key. Obviously occupied, heavy thumping music throbbed from the apartment only to be silenced by the thick walls of the old building when I moved a few steps away.

The next door was a double wood affair with a half round top, etched glass panels, and stained glass. It let us into a musty, swampy garden open to the sky. We picked our way through a mess of pots and broken trellis to another door. This lock opened freely and let us into the flat.

The first room must have been the kitchen or a part of the stables where the horses and carriages were washed because a long, low marble trough with a hand pump ran along one wall. Fortunately a stove, frige, and regular sink shared the rest of the space with a washing machine, a defunct dishwasher, and a worn table. This turned out to be the largest room in the apartment.

From the kitchen we walked into a long hallway. A hat rack with long pegs meant for top hats shared space with an ancient wardrobe and modern coat rack. Halfway down the hall another double door with stained glass on the right opened into the interior garden with its stinky pots. To the left was a long narrow sitting room.

Bright from the hanging lamp in the center of the high ceiling it was an inviting space except for the rock hard couch along one wall. Paintings of Florentine landscapes covered most of one wall. A ceiling high double door opened into the walled garden at the back of the palace. Set into the back wall of the building it revealed the massive thickness of the walls.

Two small bedrooms opened out from the narrow living room. Each bedroom also had a tall double door opening to the garden. Stained and etched glass of red and yellow with red painted shutters for night time privacy.

The garden itself was enclosed with a high wall barely revealing the dome of the old synagogue on the other side. A fountain with a statue of Cerces topped by a dog statue flanked by two eagles faced the back of the Palace.

As the week progressed I got used to threading my way through multiple locked doors to leave and enter the apartment. The lack of hot water in the kitchen was a bigger obstacle, but heating water on the stove to wash dishes soon became a normal part of the routine. The tiny bathroom with the cracked toilet seat was a tougher obstacle. The damp cold of the whole place was the biggest problem. Or so I thought.

The twenty foot ceiling in my bedroom was covered with a Japanese fresco that continued on down the walls to about eye level. A branch of cherry blossoms against a solid blue background made the ceiling and upper walls a feast of pink, white, blue, and brown. Detailed borders followed the vault of the ceiling and divided the scenes of people working on a river bank and white cranes hunting their fishy dinner in the blue water.

It was a beautiful thing, fresh and bright as the day it was painted a hundred years earlier. Until you reached the level about ten feet above the floor. The great flood of 1966 had reduced the art work below that level to a flaking, peeling shadow of the original.

It also served as a reminder that the raging Arno River had filled that room nearly full. Maybe the Fra Filippo Lippi etching of the Madonna over the head of the bed was there for a reason.

As the rainy season descended on Florence, I turned my attention to the sights within easy walking distance to our Palace. The Uffizi Gallery, Santa Croce, The Duomo, the City Market, the Academy Art Gallery, the Medici chapel, and San Lorenzo. The list was long.

A few weeks later we made a weekend trip to Rome where sunshine and warmer temperatures reigned. On our return to the Palace our front door refused to open. It had rained so hard that the central courtyard had filled with water and swelled our door shut. The landlord came and beat on the 120 year old door until it opened.

Terrible thunder and rain over the next few days made excursions difficult. With no television or radio to enlighten me about the possibility of more flooding I worried a bit more each day. After a particularly fierce storm I walked over to the Arno River to see its condition for myself. It seemed like everyone else in town had the same idea.

The police with their distinct caped uniforms were busy keeping traffic moving. Hoards of sight seers lined the river bank. The Arno was very high and running fast. Muddy and loaded with trash, the water swirled and eddied at warp speed, but it was still contained within its banks. The piers of the Ponte Vecchio were nearly obscured by the piles of junk from upstream.

On the way home I paid a visit to the refectory of Santa Croce where one of the most famous victims of the flood of 1966, Cimabue's Crucifixion, was on display. The nearly destroyed art work of 1265 A.D. was a monument to the frailty of man's work. Though painstakingly restored, Cimabue's work still looked like the lower part of the fresco over my bed at the Palace.

As the time for our departure got closer, the weather improved. I made numerous forays from the apartment to buy souvenirs and presents for friends back in the states. Antique shops, flea markets, street hucksters, the gift shops of the many museums and even churches and monasteries were good hunting grounds.

I checked on the river whenever I was in that neighborhood. It still ran fast and seemed to inch higher each day, fed by upstream rains. Higher ground still sounded good, but we had a three day stop in Venice before we headed home.

The day we bid the Palace goodbye, public transportation workers decided to strike. Our train trip to Venice turned into a bus trip about the halfway mark. We rode through miles of flooded countryside before we entered soggy Venice.

The flight to Amsterdam was short and uneventful. The first newspaper we found reported a major flood in Florence the day we left. The palace was in grave danger, but we were on our way home.

Light Bulbs and Lions

You would think that changing a light bulb would be a simple task. Not so at the Palace in Florence, Italy. Actually our part of the Palace was the converted scullery on the ground floor. The real palace was up a twenty foot spiral stair near the street entrance.

Still, our scullery apartment had fifteen foot ceilings, stained glass doors, and frescoes from the late 1800's. What it didn't have was hot water in the kitchen, heat, and a decent bathtub.

We had been living in the scullery apartment for several weeks when the light bulb in the kitchen burned out. That should have been a simple matter. It wasn't. The ceiling bulb was still many feet out of reach when I stood on a chair, so I climbed the spiral stair to the landlady's floor. I explained the problem and expected a helping hand or at least a ladder and a replacement bulb.

I'll call an electrician said the landlady. To change a light bulb? I answered. Never mind. I'll figure it out. He can probably come out tomorrow she said.

I spent the better part of the afternoon searching the nearby and not so nearby stores for a light bulb. No luck. They didn't seem to sell such things here. Some sort of ploy by the electricians union I surmised.

The next day the electrician showed up at my door with a ladder and a tool box. He climbed up and removed the old bulb, looked it over and said he'd be back on Friday. Then Friday turned out to be some sort of church holiday and our electrician was the praying sort. This was going to be one expensive light bulb.

By Monday I was seriously considering a move to another apartment. Maybe one without all the historical touches. And working light bulbs.

At noon the landlady showed up at my door with the electrician in tow. After a heated discussion in Italian the landlady climbed up the ladder and the electrician handed her the new bulb which she screwed into place.

There, she said. That saves us the trouble of filling out the paperwork for the history preservation people.

How did the city of lions sink so low? Become so trapped in rules and regulations?

It seems like there was a lion on every corner in Florence. Two standing lions guard the clock at the Palazzo Vecchio. Sitting lions holding the shield bearing the lily of Florence appear at every turn. A lion wearing a bronze crown stands in the Medici Tomb. One rather bedraggled plaster lion holds the sign pointing to the 'toilettes' at city hall. Another holds a weather vane.

When the original art work is safely locked up or ensconced in a museum, a copy fills the bill. There is even a street named the avenue of lions, the 'via dei Leoni.' Apparently this grew out of the cages of live lions kept in various locations in Florence. The first recorded example of 'lion keeping' dates from the 13th Century. As many as 25 lions were recorded at the peak of lion keeping in the 15th Century.

It seems that lions as the symbol of the free Republic of Florence trump the imperial eagle. Florence was thumbing its nose at the rest of the world.

And what has all this lion business to do with light bulbs? Not much other than to define the peculiar Italian personality that sometimes shines through the most unlikely citizen of Florence. Perhaps a few lions wandering the streets would put light bulbs in perspective. Or maybe the lights would drive the lions away.

Vikings In Szeged

In 1985 Hungary was still firmly under the control of the Soviet Union. The usual gray pall of the Communist regime with its shortages and prohibitions muffled the city of Szeged, a city that sits astraddle of the Tisza River in south eastern part of Hungary.

Amusements of the usual sort were lacking. Movies and TV were heavily censored. The only English language paper was a two page affair that appeared on the news stand sporadically. The three American students I knew about were so up to their eyeballs with school work and coping with the living conditions that they were unavailable for any socializing. My husband had enough work to keep him busy most of the time. I spent my time exploring the city.

While poking about in the gardens behind the city museum, I found a strange boat. It rested on two stone bases a dozen feet apart. Covered with briars and morning glory vine it seemed more trash than exhibit. A bit of flotsam with no clear purpose. Another interloper in a closed society.

The park was home to several large statues of royalty of a long gone era. One princess in an elaborate gown guarded the gravel path, another held court near the rubbish bins. The gardener carefully raked around them with his twig broom. It was a daily part of his job as attested to by the swirls in the dirt. No such attention was given to the old boat. It was nearly obscured by vegetation and had graffiti instead of a placard of origin.

Perhaps it really was garbage, something destined for the city dump in the years before the Soviets. Something that hadn't quite made it to the disposal site before the change of governments.

Someone had built a cabin of sorts on the boat and many of the side boards were modern day planed lumber. Parts of the boat had been painted a vicious green color. What set it apart from trash was its carved prow. The tight scroll reared back like the neck of a high strung horse and every line of the old vessel led to that point. No amount of degradation could hide the pride that produced that wooden bow.

I tried to ask the attendants at the museum about the boat, but found no one that understood my question. English speakers in a country where English had been banned from the schools since 1956 was like plucking needles from a haystack. About all I could do was pay the old vessel a visit now and then.

Years later I learned that not all Vikings were warriors seeking to plunder and burn though their more placid farmer counterparts usually began their resettlement with the expected violence. In Hungary they met up with the Magyar hoards from the east and a number of battles resulted. The flat lands of what was eventually to become Hungary were much in dispute.

Most of the invaders came via the land route, but the Vikings had a super highway down the broad, placid Tisza. A portage from the River Dnieper to the head waters of the Tisza would have brought the invaders to Szeged as would an upstream journey from the Danube in the south. Was the old boat part of a Viking flotilla? It was possible, but was it probable?

Severe flooding inundated that part of Hungary in the spring of 1879. The Danube flowed so high that it forced the Tisza to flow backwards into its own course and destroy the city of Szeged. A small wooden boat would hardly survive when the nearby cathedral was leveled.

Perhaps that the elegant prow was somehow found in the muck and debris of the ruined city and affixed to a local fisherman's craft. Perhaps. Perhaps. Another unanswered question.

The Three Line System

Brno, Czechoslovakia 1985. Except for the cathedral the churches are locked and boarded up. Stores have lines of shoppers waiting for their turn inside. Very few cars are out and about the cobblestone streets other than a few delivery vans and military vehicles. A sort of gray aura hangs over the city.

Still the most heavenly aroma comes from coffee shops and bakeries. Chocolate and espresso. One bakery displays a basket of green frosted cookies in the shape of dragons, the symbol of Brno. The cookies do look more like comic book alligators, but who is to judge.

I get in line out on the street. Only a few baskets at the entrance to the shop is a sign that it may be a long wait. Only a certain number of shoppers are allowed into the shops and this is very efficiently controlled by making it mandatory to carry basket when inside. When my turn comes I pick up a basket and enter the store. A blast of overheated air smacks me in the face.

The rule seems superfluous for so small a store, but, then, rules are rules. We edge along the cases displaying all manner of baked goods. Patrons are shouting their orders to the sweating, bandana wearing women behind the counter as we make our way towards the cashier at the end. I quickly figure out that I have no choice but to choose something near the cashier. No dragons for me.

I point to a bin of cookies and hold up four fingers. The clerk and the cashier have a quick exchange of words. The cookies are counted out, wrapped in paper and tied with string. I hold out a wad of small bills and a palm full of change to the cashier. She carefully sorts out the necessary payment and hands me a scrap of paper with the written order. A third clerk beckons me past the cashier and hands me the wrapped cookies. My first encounter with the three line system. And the easiest since it all plays out in that small contained space. The next one will be much harder.

I decide I need a scarf. It is August, but the winds have been fierce and I intend to be in Eastern Europe until December. Sometimes packing light has it disadvantages.

Unlike the bakery, the clothing store is huge and almost devoid of goods. A few ancient manikins display drab business suits for men and woman. The rest of the store is divided into sections with crude wooden counters in front of stacked drawers and cubby hole shelves. The obligatory baskets sit just past the manikins.

The first thing I must do is figure out which section sells scarves. With no display to guide me I single out the least formidable clerk and attempt a little pantomime. I slide the handle of my basket to the crook of my arm and pretend donning and tying a scarf over my head. The clerk almost smiles and leads me to a counter in the rear of the store. She hands me over to the scarf clerk with an unintelligible explanation and a duplication of my pantomime.

The clerk does not bother asking me anything. Smart lady. Instead she turns to her wall of shelves and selects a half dozen scarves. She watches intently while I examine them. One is huge and filmy, another just a narrow strip of brown knit material. Several more looked like faded cotton. I finally select a conservative green scarf with a gold and red edge. It must be wool I think. And the size is right. Who knows how much it costs because I can't read the label. I hope this isn't some high end French thing that will empty my pocket book and make me cringe every time I use it.

The clerk gives me the slip of paper that records the sale and I take it to the cashier. Meanwhile the first clerk folds and wraps the scarf in paper that looks like newsprint, then ties it with string. I didn't know it then, but later I realize there is no, nada, zero tape in this country. No plastic bags either.

The cashier takes my money and hands me another slip of paper. When I stand there looking stupid or lost or something, she points to another clerk on down the line. Apparently my wrapped scarf journeyed from station one, behind the money lady's position to yet another clerk who stands waiting for me to present this latest bit of paper. I give her a short Japanese style bow and she places my purchase in my basket.

At the door I stack my basket with the others and merge into the stream of pedestrians hurrying to find some scarce item or another. No wonder shopping becomes a priority activity under the three line system.

Two Women On A Beijing Street

A hot, June wind, armed with gritty dust, blasted a city on the far side of the world. I watch two women approach from opposite sides of a cluttered sidewalk near the Forbidden City. I imagine they had never met before, and after this brief interval, they would not meet again.

I call the first woman, Kuoug Soon, a small woman, all shuffling feet and flapping sleeves. Her jet hair streaked with white is pulled tight behind her ears in a hard twist. A woven bamboo coolie hat sucked at her head, its chin chord biting at her sunken cheeks. She holds a covered bird cage by the silver ring wired to its rusty top. The ancient crone gives no sign that her knobbed, crooked fingers ache as they grasp the slender handle. Her old style Mao suit with its shapeless, faded tunic and loose pajama-like trousers enfold her spare body. Only her obsidian eyes and crinkled grin contradict her dusty grayness.

The second woman, let's call her Silvia Shane, is smooth and new. A tall, tanned, willowy, young Canadian, she wears gold sandals and a 'little' dress of lime green cotton. Her long, ashy-blond hair falls heavy around her bare shoulders, drawing the attention of sidewalk loungers and quick moving pedestrians alike.

Face-to-face on the cracked, ragged sidewalk, the two women stop and stared at one-another. Quick as smoke, the old woman holds up the bird cage, then whips off its cover. The tiny bird inside puffs up its blond ruff and burst into song. Enchanted, the tall girl listens with her hands folded, loose and graceful, across her breasts. When the bird finishes its song, the old woman replaces the cover and disappears down a narrow ally of over-hanging tin roofs. The stench of a public toilet mixes with the tang of heating cooking oil at the Dum Sin Restaurant on the corner.

As the old woman disappears down the dirty ally, Silvia realizes they had attracted a crowd of curious people. One bystander in particular, a Chinese man with a thin goatee catches her eye. The bystander wears a custom suit of shiny, pin-stripe serge and mirror-finish wing-tip shoes, perfect, spotless against the background of the street. He gestures to Silvia as soon as he sees the flapping woman with the bird disappear down the alley.

Standing before her on the pavement, he wrings his hands together at chest level, then pretends to eat. He concludes his mock meal by licking his fingers and delicately probing a back tooth for invisible particles. Silvia stares at the man's antics, not quite comprehending his meaning. With a frown he swaggers up and down the pavement, thrusting his hips out to pantomime the expected result of eating the songbird with lewd reality. Silvia gasps at this new reality and stumbles back to the hotel, disgusted and diminished.

On The Trail of an Artist

1985 Budapest was a pretty gray place. Goods were scarce and many small shops were long closed. One such place was just off my usual path through downtown Budapest. It must have been an antique shop or a junk store before the war and communist occupation. Peering through the filthy windows revealed a collection of old brass lamps, small end tables, china bowls, stem ware, souvenirs from a long forgotten world fair, rotting dresses with feather boas on a tilted rack. Dark paintings hung crookedly on the peeling walls. All treasures of a kinder era.

In the window sat a ceramic figure unlike any I had ever seen. Under a thick coat of dust a statue of a woman or an angel with a trumpet and flowing hair, sleeves, and long robe presided over gangs of cheap glass animals and plastic toys. The figure was thrown on a wheel and then modified with clay added to form its head, arms, and trumpet. The brown clay was decorated with a coat of slip to color the dress blue, hands and face a pale pink, then glazed and fired. This was not a mass produced knick-knack or some art school project gone awry.

Each time I passed that way, I checked to see if anything had changed, if the shop keeper had returned, or the shop reopened, but nothing. I put the thought of learning more or acquiring the figure out of my mind when I left the country at Christmas time.

On a visit sixteen years later I found Budapest much changed. It was like a room where the lights had been turned on and everything dusted and polished. The old antique shop had vanished to make way for a boutique clothing store. No one knew where the contents of the shop had ended up, but someone thought an auction had been held.

Later I showed a sketch I had made of the figure to several local friends. One thought it looked like some of the pottery displayed in a nearby town. The next day I took the tram to Szentendre. There my sketch was met with nods, smiles, and fingers directing me to a narrow street off the main drag. After some wandering I found a big stucco building with a sign on the front with a depiction of a potter at work and a name—Kovacs Margit. Margit Kovacs, an artist of stature, yet I had never heard of her in all my studies in art history.

The sign and a large ceramic figure standing guard told me I was at the right place. Inside a guard informed me 'no photos allowed.' A woman seated at a desk gave me a thin paper ticket the size of a postage stamp in return for the admission price of a few Forints—about fifty cents.

The building may have been the home of the potter long ago. A studio complete with several potter's wheels, clay working tools, and a brick kiln shared space with shelves of unfired work.

As I moved into the museum proper the displays were more artful. Single figures on pedestals, groups in glass cases, large pieces adorning the walls and corners. The work of a life time. Who was this woman?

Ten years later I was in Gyor, a town near Hungary's border with Austria, when I heard that this was Margit Kovac's birthplace. After asking directions from numerous shop keepers I was directed to a long two story flat iron style building. An apothecary and a restaurant occupied the ground floor, but I finally found an entrance to the second floor with a sign indicating a Muemlek or museum. A second sign read Kovacs Margit Gyujemeny. 'Gyujemeny,' that unspellable, unpronounceable word means 'collection.'

The entrance led to a steep narrow stairway that ascended to a bright room that ran the length of the building. Some sixty-five ceramic pieces by Margit Kovacs were displayed there.

I approached the lady at the desk to pay the entrance fee. In addition I asked if I could get permission to take photographs. That proved to be far more complicated. And expensive. I filled out several forms which I couldn't read, signed them, and paid a fee of about twenty dollars. It was well worth it.

Any one of a dozen art pieces could have been the one in that long ago dusty window in Budapest. Angels, trumpeters, mothers, children, fairy tale characters, folk lore heroes had spun from Margit's fingers as she sat at her potter's wheel. It was an awesome display.

Then I found the trumpeter from long ago. He was labeled 'The Angel Gabriel.' He had found a suitable home far better than a shelf in my house. I bought a book with the life story of the artist and many pictures, including the angel Gabriel. Close enough.

Romanian Recycling

When I get tired of the usual recycling drill of check label, sort, rinse, and flatten before tossing the weekly accumulation into the recycling bins, I think of the recycling going on in the old part of Cluj-Napoca, Romania.

I was staying at the Agape Hotel just off the main square. My room had a good view of the busy intersection below. Pedestrians, delivery vans, cars, and an occasional horse drawn wagon moved through the area from early to late.

One morning I noticed a hotel employee stacking card board cartons from the kitchen, boxes of paper, and plastic bottles on the curb near the corner. Over the next few days the stack grew higher and wider until it was hard to walk past it or to park in the spaces nearby.

No one bothered the pile. Not the passing walkers nor the homeless who slept in a nearby churchyard. The pile was carefully constructed and never wavered even when it grew more than head high.

On Friday a man with a large handcart showed up. Not the puny handcart we see in big box stores or lumber yards, but a giant with two rubber automobile tires and a handle built for pulling or pushing. The fellow looked small next to the pile, but he was strong. He spent the morning loading the pile onto his cart.

After a morning's work the tower of cardboard and paper was stacked on the teetering cart. The young man used a rope and a netting to secure the load, then put every ounce of his muscle into getting the cart in motion. With a bit of a struggle to get his load off the curb he pushed it down the middle of the street, oblivious of the traffic which parted around him.

I saw him several times that Friday, each time with a different load gathered from the shops and restaurants in the old town.

If the pioneers had had recycling this would be it.

Climbing Cologne

The Cathedral tower of course. All 533 steps of it.

The cathedral itself is 515 feet tall. One of the tallest cathedrals in Europe, it was begun in 1248 and finished after many halts and glitches in 1880. When you arrive in Cologne and step off the train it hits you like some enormous eruption smack in the center of town.

When I found that climbing the south tower was allowed, I knew that was the next event in my life. My husband declined and wandered off to look at ground level sights. October 1990 and no admission charge or ticket was required, so I entered the narrow stone framed doorway to the tower. It was like a dim culvert with a tight winding spiral stair of stone steps.

The steps were taller than normal stairs and the first seventy feet or so the spiral was very tight. About thirty feet above ground level I heard a commotion of voices and feet from below and a few seconds later a gang of school boys stormed the tower. I leaned back against the wall and let them squeeze past. Their footsteps and high pitched chatter echoed through the tower until they reached the bells. I was barely at the 100 foot level when they charged back down. They were the only people I met in the tower. How could this place stand an onslaught of tourists?

As I moved upward and the tower widened, windows began appearing in the outside wall. At first they were small and set high in the wall, but as I continued they grew until they reached the floor. No glass in these openings of course, but the first few had metal grills over them. The farther up the tower I went, the more flimsy the wire grills became. Some were bent up and outward and brought to mind accidents and suicides. A misstep and it would be all over. The square below was a very long way down.

When I reached the bell level, a new worry occurred to me. What if these gigantic bells rang while I stood there gawking at them. And those ringers—they were big as babies and hung down a couple of feet below the edge of the bell. There was no railing to keep observers away so it looked like you could get a good clout if you stood too close during the ringing.

But the view of the square below was spectacular. All of Cologne spread out below. Way below.

The next part of the climb was up an open steel stairway. Wider with more normal steps, but in its own sweet way just as scary.

By the time I stopped to look down on the bells I was exhausted. Fortunately step 533 was near. With shaky knees I touched the stone wall at the end of the upward passage. A few brave souls had scratched initials and messages on the wall. One of them read 'Never Again.' Another said 'Heaven is nigh.' Close enough anyway.

I took some photos, then scrambled, staggered, and slid back down those 533 steps to Mother Earth. Safe again.

Leaving Lviv

The airport was just outside of town. A few buildings in need a coat of paint and a good cleaning on the edge of a circle drive. Inside a crowd of noisy people waited for the two gates to clear for the next flights out. A flight from Lviv to Vienna. And one to Prague.

Security was something out of the past. A hulking man in uniform spent many minutes swiveling his stare between me and my passport photo, then nodded me through to the security check.

No machines, no x-ray, no nothing except another uniform and his probing fingers. He began at my hair line and worked his way downward. Sifted through the contents of my pockets, my waist pack, shoes, socks. When he was satisfied with his search of my person, he turned to my backpack. No wonder the line moved so slow.

Things were quiet in the waiting lounge. The forty or so people who had made it through the security bottleneck talked a bit, checked and rechecked their tickets, repacked bags and back packs. Then a flight delay was announced and lines formed at the rest rooms. The Ukraine was not finished with us.

As I waited my turn, the ladies exiting the toilets jabbered loudly to anyone or no one. One flung up her hands and made obscene gestures towards the main hall. Another ducked into the rest room and returned immediately holding a handkerchief over her face. The mother behind me picked up her crying toddler and returned to the waiting lounge.

These signs of trouble gave me pause when my turn came. The large room was bright with a wall of windows, new fixtures, tile floor, a half dozen stalls, and a layer of crap over everything. Piles in the corners, puddles oozing out from under the stall doors. I backed out as quickly as I could without knocking anyone down.

I returned to my seat and began weighing the pros and cons of leaving the airport in search of a fresher toilet against having to go through security again plus the danger of missing my flight. Someone said the plane was now an hour behind schedule, so I made my way out of the airport and followed some people across the square to a small building attached to a defunct night club. There was a sign outside that read 'free toilet.'

They should have paid people to go inside.

A woman was seated at the restroom door. She held up her palm and traced a number. The price for the use of the 'free' facilities. I gave her the coin and she handed me a small wad of folded tissue.

It turned out to be a pit toilet in a closet sized room in back. No light, no sink. Thwarted again. When I immediately reappeared, the attendant took pity on me and led me to another, larger room equipped with all the comforts expected by us spoiled travelers.

A light that worked and a door. No lock, but no matter. A real actual toilet with a seat even. A small sink with cold water and a faucet. And it was clean.

On my way out I gave the attendant a hug and a ten dollar bill. Now we were both happy. Across the street at the airport I even managed a smile for the fellow at security and he actually smiled back and waved me through without a pat down.

Passengers were just lining up to board the flight when I returned. Could the glitter of Vienna be any better?

Tram 18

September in Budapest is a golden time. Today, the feeble light of early morning paints sidewalks, store fronts, and crusted monuments a bright ochre. The air of Gellert ter is a mingle of exhaust fumes from buses and cast off American cars with the warm aroma of fresh bread streaming from the below street bakery.

I stand at the curb and watch the silent trams glide in and out. The steep escalators from the underground metro spit out office workers, clerks, students, and shoppers with their knit bags that will soon bulge with cabbage, bread, fat salami, paprika.

Trying to blend with the crowd are the gaggles of refugees come to take up their posts for the day. Dressed mostly in black or gray, they stand elbow to elbow the required ten feet from the metro ticket windows. They are selling all manner of stuff. They either hold items out to those who pass by or leave it piled at their feet to leave their hands free to can catch a sleeve or an elbow of a passing customer. Wooden toys, cheap lighters, and spray deodorant, flowers, embroidered cloths.

Two professors from the nearby Technical University stand beside me at the tram stop. One is most certainly a local, a Hungarian, bred and born in the Buda hills. Perhaps he is descended from the original merchants who traveled here to the broad Danube to buy and sell in the shadow of Buda Castle. Or, maybe he claims some ancient denizen of the castle itself, a potter or a prince, bard, or scribe, for his ancestor. His head is bent over a worn book, which, to my surprise, is a Hungarian translation of *Huckleberry Finn*.

The other gentleman is English or American. American, I think. The faded blue jeans are the tip off. Hungarians are still a fastidious race and seldom appear on the street in casual clothing.

He pages through a newspaper, rumpling more than reading. With a flourish he dumps the wadded mess on the bench behind me. It is last week's English edition of the *Daily News*.

"Tram 18. Where the hell is tram 18?"

The American looks at the Hungarian, but clearly aims his complaint at me. I smile and shake my head. He looks anxiously up and down the track.

"Damn these trams. Schedules don't mean much around here."

The Hungarian edges away, turns his shoulder to deflect the loud words, and holds his book higher.

The American rummages in his backpack, then confronts the Hungarian.

"Do you speak English?"

"Most certainly. I speak English, thank you," replies the Hungarian.

He lowers his book with a sigh, then settles his hat more firmly on his head. Hands clasped around his book, he murmurs something in Hungarian, then stands silent.

I watch the American pace up and down the sidewalk. He stops and faces us.

"Can you tell me how these trams are guided?"

Nose to nose, now, he repeats his question. "How, man? How do they work?"

He has the Hungarian cornered in the shelter now. He pantomimes a tram sliding into the stop, easing from the curb, switching tracks, and gliding away. His voice rises to a near shout and I wonder why people think they will be understood if they speak louder.

"I don't see anyone throwing switches or operating a steering mechanism. Tram 18 travels the track along the Danube to Moszkva ter and then Tram 48 comes on the same track, makes a right-hand turn, and crosses the river to the Pest side."

"Yes, yes," says the Hungarian.

"These Russian-made trams are a mystery to me."

The American kneels on the dusty cobblestones trying to peer underneath Tram 53 as it jerks to a stop.

"However do they get these things to go in the right direction?"

"Yes," says the Hungarian.

"So. Can you shed some light on this?" He brushes the dust from his jeans.

"Tram 18 will be here in ten minutes."

"No. No. How do they steer the trams?"

"Ten minutes, sir," says the Hungarian. "We have very good trams here."

"Steer. Turn corners." He mimics turning a steering wheel.

"Tram 18 will be here in ten minutes."

"Steer, steer. Who drives the tram?" He turns his imaginary wheel, pulls an invisible bell rope.

The Hungarian turns to a fellow commuter, shrugs, points to his head, and walks away.

Mount Moriah

Mt. Moriah Cemetery in Deadwood South Dakota is known as a part of the city's tourist attractions, but it also draws the local residents. Some come to gawk and take pictures, others have had more nefarious motives, namely souvenir collecting and outright vandalism.

The main attraction is the grave of Wild Bill Hickok, but numerous other old time Deadwood citizens are also buried here. Calamity Jane, Seth Bullock, Rev. Henry Weston Smith, and Potato Creek Johnny reside here.

Getting to the cemetery is not an easy task because it is high on a bluff above the business district of town. A female mountaineer-type woman tried to scale the bluff one year and required a rescue team to get her down.

Nowadays a black top road snakes up the low side of the bluff, then bends back on itself to enter the cemetery through a wrought iron gate. At least it looks like iron. It could be some light weight material devised by modern alchemy. The original gate was taken in one of the scrap metal drives for World War II.

Our treks up the bluff to visit Wild Bill and friends began in the early 1940's. It was war time and most of the men were off in strange faraway places for the Army and Navy. The women and children left behind often devised some rather odd ways of amusing themselves.

Mt. Moriah by far was the most exciting and challenging of those amusements. Getting an ancient cranky car up that steep slippery gravel and bare rock road involved a lot of shifting and cursing. My mom was new to driving and the car was on its last legs. Alternately gunning the engine, shifting, then high centering on a slab of rock made the trip hair raising. Coming back down was easier. Take the car out of gear and coast, but keep your foot on the brake pedal. Run off the road and you'd probably land on someone's roof.

When we finally arrived on the top, we were greeted with a majorly spectacular view of the town and the surrounding countryside. Most of the graves were still unfenced at that time and we would spread a blanket on old Wild Bill's grave and eat our picnic lunch. For variety we would climb up the hill towards White Rocks and eat on the grave of Seth Bullock, first sheriff in Deadwood. He died in 1919. Our family album has photos of us kids sitting on his tombstone.

A more recent addition to Mt. Moriah was the burial of Potato Creek Johnny in 1943. He was famous for finding a huge gold nugget in 1929. In the weeks before his death he had been one of my mother's patients at St. Joseph Hospital just up the highway from the turnoff to Mt. Moriah. He was past saving when he finally went to see a doctor according to my mom who worked as a nurse. Potato Creek Johnny was buried next to Wild Bill and Calamity Jane.

A statue of Wild Bill had been had been placed on his plot in 1902, but vandals and souvenir hunters had chipped away on it year after year until was finally removed to a museum. No doubt we were partially responsible. Even though many of the graves had been fenced over the years, it was little bother to climb over, go around, or breech those fences. We did it regularly.

When the war ended and husbands and brothers came home, we had celebrations, job and house hunting, general readjustments. We scattered across the country to make our futures secure. Our visits to Mt. Moriah ceased.

Some sixty or seventy years passed before I returned to Deadwood. The town had changed drastically with the downtown being a solid line of casinos from one end to the other. Wild Bill would have loved this new Deadwood, but I wanted to find a grocery store and a druggist somewhere in this sea of slots and gaming tables.

After a good, but futile search I asked a skinny teenager if he knew where to buy potato chips. And soda. He said the town's only super market had closed the year before and directed me to the back room of one of the gambling palaces where I found a corner devoted to junk food and various canned drinks.

I carried my purchases back to my hotel room, a room that was a strange mix of old and new. Heavy satin curtains, a tall bed heaped with comforters, antique, or at least old, tables, dresser, and faded pictures next to a flat screen TV. No telephone or internet connection. Some of the rooms had old claw foot bathtubs, but I lucked out with a brand new shower and thick towels. The room key probably had some of Wild Bill's dried sweat on it. No matter. A firm slap on the door frame opened the door without the key.

The next day I took one of the shuttle tours that touted their wares on main street. About all it promised was a good view of the canyon and a visit to Wild Bill's grave, but then it only cost twenty-five bucks. The open-sided bus sat at the curb until it had accumulated enough passengers, then lurched its way up the bluff.

At the gate the driver stopped and did a head count, then paid the two dollars per person admission. Admission to a graveyard? He drove a short distance to a narrow blacktop space with a bus only parking sign and stopped. We were still a flight of concrete steps from the top. With much huffing and complaining the tour group followed the driver up the hill.

The driver was also our guide and a fifth grade teacher in the local school. He proved to be both knowledgeable and nice. While he recounted the history of Deadwood, I got a good look around. It seemed like most of the graves had been cemented over and sturdy fences kept us in line. Signs informed and directed and made our old quarrels over which grave held whose bones obsolete. Most of the old markers had been moved to the local museum and new copies adorned the place. Ditto the busts and full size statuary. Only the view over the canyon seemed untouched. The aspen and birch were a shimmering yellow against the evergreens clear to the horizon.

We had a short tour and a good lecture on the history of the place, then were allowed some time to wander around by ourselves. I went back to Mr. Bullocks grave. They must have moved him because the location was unfamiliar. Much closer to the edge of the bluff. When the tour guy came by I asked him about it. He consulted a worn book and decided it must be true. Moving the grave saved the gawkers and the cemetery workers a long hike over treacherous rocks.

As we walked back to the bus, I mentioned my childhood exploits in the cemetery to our guide. I pulled a piece of white granite in a baggie from my pocket. I showed it to the guide and told him that the piece of stone came from Seth Bullock's headstone in 1943.

He examined the rock, a rock polished on two sides, chisel marks on the other. Definitely an edge piece he said. You kept this all these years. It was a reminder I told him. A reminder to come back one day. You can keep it.

Leaving Budapest 1990

On October 23, 1989 the Hungarians voted themselves out of the Soviet Union and ended the long occupation of their country. There had been no bullets, no riots, no fighting, no marches, just a simple vote. Unfortunately the transition to come did not go as smoothly.

We arrived in Budapest in September of 1990 just in time for one of the transition glitches. We stayed the first night at our favorite hotel on the bank of the Danube, then spent most of the next day taking care of the necessary paper work for a semester stay. We had been assigned a guide for the day. He showed us how the metro system worked, got us passes for the month and turned us loose to find our way to our new apartment.

When we exited the Moszkva ter metro station, we were met by a wall of horn honking. A hundred or more taxi drivers were driving the circular road around the station. Windows rolled down and shaking their raised fists, the drivers shouted the space between the horns full with unintelligible complaints and demands. Fortunately for us not all the taxis were engaged with protesting and we found a willing driver in the taxi line.

The driver helped us load our backpacks into the trunk and took off. We made one circle of the metro station and headed up the long steep hill to our new apartment.

"What's going on?"

"Those damn Soviets," said the driver.

"What about them. I thought Hungary voted out the Socialist Workers Party last fall?"

"Damn Russians raised the price of gas. Don't like us having free elections."

And raised the price indeed. The old subsidized price of a few cents a gallon was now as high as any fuel in either Western or Eastern Europe. Before the price change Taxi drivers had been close to elite status for income. Now they were struggling to survive. But could you blame the Russians?

Our apartment was near the crest of the hill on a street named Galgoczy which we called Goat Street. It was a far piece from almost everything. The view was spectacular, but the metro was more than a mile down hill and two up. A decent grocery store was even farther.

After a few days we found a bus that toiled up and down our hill between the hill top and the metro. The bus drivers were threatening to join the taxi drivers in sympathy so our transportation link was short lived.

We went about our business for a few weeks, then a planned free election fired a new round of protest. The first anniversary of Hungary's declaration of freedom added to the unrest.

We were due to move to Szeged at the end of October so on the 26th my husband made the three hour train trip to haul the bulk of our belongings to our apartment there. I spent the day watching the growing protests on the TV and listening to the sounds of the uproar that drifted up the hill.

As the time for his return passed, my worry grew. Late that night he made it up the hill on foot. The Metro was still running, but all other transportation in the city had come to a screeching halt. The bridges were blocked with 'borrowed' delivery trucks.

The train had been very late because a car had been placed across the tracks in an attempt to halt it. It did stop, but a group of young men jumped off and finally managed to move the car to the side. The train proceeded into Budapest very slowly.

The next morning, Saturday October 27, we knew we had to get out of Budapest. The stores were already empty of staples like bread, milk, and fresh produce. The lines were long. Strikers threatened to close all border crossings. All major highways were blocked.

We called a friend with a car and begged a ride to the Moszkva ter metro station. From there we rode to the Kelletti train station. We hoped to get a train to Vienna. The station was jammed full of people with similar goals. Protesters mobbed the train and declared they would close down the whole country including the border crossings.

We shared a compartment with an Indian from Deli, but living in Paris, a French tourist who managed to sleep all the way to Vienna, and an Austrian businessman who had abandoned his car on a Budapest street. The guy from Deli and the Austrian argued the merits of the Hungarian people all the way to the border crossing. The Indian was very angry, but the Austrian worked hard to convince him that the Hungarians were very nice people to do business with. Seems he was an exporter of Hungarian fruit juices.

At the border we were stopped for a long time but eventually continued on to Vienna. It was the last train out of Hungary that week. The strike was complete.

We had a couple of great days in Vienna, then traveled to Venice and on to several other European cities. The contrast of staid, civil Western Europe with unruly Hungary was night and day.

Ten days later the newspaper reports finally let us know that Hungary had cooled off. The stores had food on their shelves and all buses, trams, and trains were operating on normal schedules. We headed back to complete our move to Szeged and to finish out the semester there.

Two Sides of the Coin

The day was bright and strangely cool for August. How far north was Moscow anyway? The pedestrian shopping street, the Arbat, teemed with shoppers, tourists, vendors, and thieves. I strolled cautiously, ignoring the sleeve tugging boys selling cheap pins and fake Red Army medals. Older boys danced in front of me offering T-shirts with Mickey Mouse at the Kremlin and faded slides of the Armory's treasures, all available at the Hotel Ukraina's gift shop for half the price.

Today, I was hunting for more substantial souvenirs. Through a break in the crowd, I noticed an old man seated on a folding stool with a small selection of coins for sale including a fine set of silver kopeks from the reign of the last czar, Nicholas II. The two headed eagles glared fiercely from the reverse of each coin when I asked, "How much?"

"Five dollars." The old man peered at me with hope in his rheumy eyes.

"Are you sure?" I asked, amazed because the set would cost much, much more in the states.

"Four dollars." Not understanding he held up four shaking fingers.

From the medals on his worn gray jacket, I knew he was a veteran living on a tiny monthly pension. He was offering a cherished family treasure in trade for a month's wage.

With hands shaking worse than the old vet's, I handed him a twenty dollar bill, accepted the packet of coins, and left before he could think about it. At the head of the lane, I looked back and answered his good-by wave. I felt like a thief.

Small Encounters
The Lady on the Bus, The Man on the Train

A lady in a turquoise coat waved to me from across Market Square. When I responded with an open mouthed stare, her waving escalated to the two armed variety more appropriate for a cheer leader. Who was this exuberant woman? I was many, many miles from home. To be exact, three plane flights, an over-night at an airport hotel, a bus ride, and a train trip away from home. After three days of travel I was now in Zilina, Slovakia hunting for fruit at the local farmer's market.

Had I seen anyone at the hotel, either staff or guest, that could have sparked this greeting? The hotel staff had been very welcoming and insisted they remembered me from a previous stay, but the blue coated woman was not one of them. Maybe she was the lady on the bus.

Mentally, I retraced my steps from the time the plane touched down at the Vienna airport. It was raining like crazy and we were all dripping wet by the time we trekked from the plane to the terminal. The NH Hotel was just across the street from the airport and a one night stay cost 122 Euros, but it was a welcome oasis, home away from home.

I spent the night at the airport hotel. After a great breakfast I returned to the airport to buy my bus ticket to Bratislava. The bus arrived on time and we lined up politely to board. It was early and everyone was quiet. The rain had stopped though and everything looked clean and bright. I took the first empty aisle seat and stuffed my bag in the overhead rack.

Just before the bus started up a tall lady with several shopping bags boarded the bus. She passed my seat and found a place near the middle section of the bus. After she stowed her bags, she came back and gestured me towards her seat. Not having a clue about what she was saying, I collected my bag and followed her. She stood aside while I slid into the window seat.

"Good," she said. "Nice view soon." She waved at the window.

She was right about the scenery that rolled past the bus as it dived into the countryside outside the airport. Rather than stick to the main highway, it trundled through one small town or village after another. I snapped pictures as my seatmate gave me warning in advance of each approaching opportunity.

At the bus stop in Bratislava we parted company. I spent a couple days doing tourist things, then got the train to Zilina in Slovakia.

The lady in the turquoise coat made her way through the crowd and hugged me. Then she waved her friends over and asked me 'photos?' I took her picture, but that wasn't what she wanted. I scrolled back to the pictures I had shot on the bus ride and handed her the camera. She showed them to the others with much explanation and giggling.

After a lot of gesturing and conversation interspersed with a few words of English I decided she wanted copies of the photos. I followed her to a nearby shop and handed the memory card to the man behind the counter. With a few quick motions he had loaded the photos to a CD and showed us how to make prints with the do-it-yourself machine.

She made copies for herself and her friends, then made sure I had the photo card re-installed in my camera. With more hugs and a kiss on each cheek we said goodbye and went our separate ways.

Another mini encounter happened on the train from Bergen to Oslo way back in 1992. My husband struck up a conversation with a local author named Terry Plant. They talked about writing and storytelling for awhile. Mr. Plant showed us some of his books and we bought several. They were the sort of stories this countryside would inspire. Steep mountains, snow clad even in July, a winding river far below, a glacier used as the setting for a Star Wars movie.

As the train slowed for a particularly steep bit of track, Mr. Plant made his way through the car peering out the windows. When he found just the right place, he motioned us to come along. We protested that we would be intruding on the people sitting in those particular seats. No problem he answered. They will be happy to share this treasure with you.

He made sure I had my camera ready. It was a short wait. The Tvinde Falls thundered into view and I snapped my pictures. Time for just two, but they proved to be as spectacular as Mr. Plant had promised. Everyone cheered. I thanked them and went back to my seat. It was a worthy end to a great train ride.

Romanian Visits: Hugs and Tears

The Wedding

Dormition of the Theotokos Church

Every few years we traveled to Cluj-Napoca, Romania for math conferences. It is a city with many fine old buildings, museums, and churches. Some of them very old and others not so much. Most of them looked rundown and uncared for, not surprising considering the history of Romania. Restoration seemed inevitable as the 20th Century came to a close.

Close to the hotel is one of the not so old churches that seemed to be going the wrong direction. Built in the years of 1923 to 1933 the Dormition of Theotokos Church was erected in the center of Avram Lancu Square. It is right across from the huge and very beautiful and very old opera house. A very tall statue of Mr. Avram presides over it all.

The name of this Eastern Orthodox church means the death or sleep of the God Bearer, Mary. Just inside the entrance is a huge mosaic depicting her passage to heaven.

This orthodox church is dark even by usual standards. Bits of building stone marked by orange cones or not at all cluttered the floor of its cavern-like interior. The central dome was reported to be on the verge of collapse. The worshipers paid no mind to the warnings. They continued to kiss pictures of saints, light candles, and pray.

Each year that I made a visit to the church, its possible collapse grew more evident. By this visit in 2012 a tall scaffolding of pipes and timbers had been erected to support the dome. Perhaps repairs were scheduled to begin soon.

Busy photographing a group of stone lions with a basin, I did not notice the sudden entrance of a wedding party. Other visitors scurried past them to exit the church. I didn't want to walk through the group of well dressed people so I slipped around the scaffolding and found a seat on a carved bench in the shadows. Perhaps leery of the weakened dome, the wedding party assembled just inside the doors at the church entrance. I later learned that a traditional Orthodox wedding always started there and moved forward in stages as the ceremony progressed. Not so this one. It remained near the entrance.

Two boys set up a table with a cross, candles, various bowls, a chalice, and a huge Bible, then disappeared into the shadows.

The bride and groom wore the usual wedding garb, black tux and long white dress. They would have fit in anywhere. The priests in their ankle length robes, gold stoles, and high hats not so much. They carried the incense and holy water. A blue jean wearing photographer hovered around the group to complete and record the event.

The ceremony began with rings and candles and a joining of hands. I snapped a few photos, then settled down to observe. Gradually I realized that the priest was repeating himself. In English. What was going on? I had heard no one in the wedding party speaking anything but Romanian before the ceremony began. Was part of the couple American or British? I watched them carefully for any sign that they were following the priest's words in English with greater understanding, but their blank stares said 'no.'

Either the priest was practicing his language skills or else he translated for my benefit. The mother of the bride looked my way and smiled. Later, on the steps outside, we hugged and she gestured to let me know that I was welcome to join the official photographer to snap a few photos.

It reminded me of the hugs and gentle acknowledgements that unite people of different cultures at big life events. One in particular.

On 9-11 we were also in Cluj. We were staying at the old Continental Hotel on the main city square. When we came back from lunch in the hotel dining room, we switched on the TV which had one channel in English, CNN. Paula Zahn and Aaron Brown were broadcasting the first footage of the 9-11 attacks on New York City. We sat on the bed and watched for the rest of the afternoon.

The next day we went back to our usual routine. When I went out on the street an old lady with worn shoes and elbow out sweater came up and hugged me. Others followed suit, many with tears in their eyes.

If you think you can blend in, become invisible outside your own bubble of culture, you are wrong. When we left Romania, we traveled a long road back to Amsterdam to get our flight home. We were lucky we had scheduled our return for early October since all flights were canceled and rebooked over and over in the weeks after 9-11 until the airlines could make up for lost time.

I met many distraught students stuck in Vienna, Prague, Rothenberg, Aachen, and Brussels. Out of cash and no way home. There was little I could do to help. There were too many of them and a little cash only gave them a meal or a cup of coffee. A silent hug was the most I could offer.